THE SECRET OF FLITTERMOUSE CLIFFS

THE SECRET OF FLITTERMOUSE CLIFFS

By

Zöe Billings

Illustrated by Sarah King

2022

ISBN: 9798834561156
Cover and internal illustrations by Sarah King
Cover layout by Zöe Billings

For Mum and Dad, and of course, to Barrie, who now lives in the pages.

My thanks to my dear proof readers who have assisted and advised throughout this second novel. Your help has been invaluable. Thanks also to Mark Pannone, for acting as technical consultant for all things involving ropes.

Contents

Chapter One

Back at Grey Owls

"And remember, no mischief!" laughed Barrie's dad, ruffling his son's fair curls as he gave him a hug.

"As if we would!" replied Barrie, adopting the most innocent facial expression he could muster. His dad, Alan, laughed again and, waving to James, got into the driver's seat of his large old Volvo and started the engine.

"I'm proud of you both!" he called, as the car pulled away and, looking in his rear-view mirror, he smiled at the disappearing image of the two boys, surrounded by bags, waving madly at him. A last wave out of the driver's window, a quick pip of his horn and he was gone, turning left out of the long driveway that belonged to Grey Owls Boarding School and disappearing down a country lane.

James grinned at Barrie and, seeing his friend's eyes glistening more than usual, thumped him gently on the arm.

"It's a bit odd after the long summer, isn't it? Suddenly being without them again. I felt like you do now yesterday. We had to come down on Saturday because of Dad's shifts, you'll soon be back in the routine."

Barrie was grateful for James' compassion. He was very close to his dad after losing his mum when he was very young and, after a summer holiday at their home in North Wales with an adventure most children only get to read about, the autumn term and dreary cold winter ahead did not seem appealing in the slightest.

James and Barrie, Bar to his friends, were both boarding school pupils at Grey Owls, deep in the heart of North Yorkshire. An imposing Victorian building built of red brick and stone, surrounded by its grounds of green fields and dense woodland, it could appear quite daunting, especially when viewed for the first time. The various knots of new year seven pupils, huddled nervously on the lawn or being gently prized away from effusive parents, were testament to how intimidating Grey Owls was to its new pupils, and Barrie couldn't help but think back a year and another lump rose in his throat.

"Come on," said James, disturbing his train of thought. "Let's get your bags to your room. There's enough here to last a whole year, never mind a term."

Barrie grabbed a case and grinned back. "I think half of it at least is baking and treats for us all from Nain! She was busy in her kitchen for days and kept saying now she has three surrogate grandchildren to cater for as well as me, she must send plenty."

Nain, the Welsh word for gran and pronounced 'nine', was one of the first Welsh words Barrie, who came from North Wales, had taught his three friends the year before.

James laughed. He, along with Jenny and Liz had loved Barrie's gran like their own when they had met her while staying at Barrie's farmhouse in the summer holidays. A fierce ally of the four, and overly generous with tasty offerings, Nain had been instrumental in the thrilling adventure the four had enjoyed when priceless silver, stolen from the nearby Tully Hall, had the police stumped as to where it was and who had stolen it.

"Your nain is an absolute treasure," said James. "My nan has also sent some packets of biscuits, so we are well catered for."

Heavily laden, they both clomped into Grey Owls through the large oak front door, their footsteps echoing loudly on the hardwood floors as they navigated the high ceilinged corridors.

"I got us rooms next to each other," said James as they entered the dormitory block. "Don't want you running into Thunder every time we want a late-night feast!"

Thunder was their nickname for Mr Storm, a fearsome teacher who patrolled the corridors and had caught both Barrie and James out past lights out in the previous terms.

"Good thinking," said Barrie, following James through a door and setting his bags down inside.

All the rooms were the same at Grey Owls, a bed, a desk with a chair and a wardrobe. "Have you heard from Jenny yet? Do you know when she's arriving?"

Jenny, whose main passion was writing stories, was a fellow boarder at Grey Owls. She had green eyes and shoulder-length brown hair, and was the only traditional boarder of the four, in the strictest sense. Barrie had a place at the school because one of his ancestors, having being a successful business owner in Yorkshire, had built it for his workers' children to attend, while James had won a science scholarship designed for pupils whose parents wouldn't normally afford the fees. Liz, the youngest of the four, attended as a day pupil, travelling in each day with her mum, Mrs Green who was the head of history, and the four's favourite teacher.

"She said she should be here by six," replied James. "If you get unpacked, we can meet her at the front, quickly get her bags in and then all go into the dining hall for tea before all the edible choices have gone."

Barrie did as he suggested and soon they were both standing by the front waiting impatiently for Jenny to appear. James, clapping his arms around himself, was regretting leaving his coat in his room. Being from Newcastle where it was normal to see people in t-shirts all year round, James was nevertheless feeling more than a little chilled stood still. It was only the first week of September but was unseasonably cold and already some of the leaves on trees were beginning to change colour.

After what seemed like forever, and a steady stream of cars depositing pupils, the boys recognised the excited face of Jenny, half hanging out of the rear passenger window as a dark 4x4 purred up the drive. Jenny jumped out almost before the car had stopped and threw herself at the boys, her green eyes shining like emeralds at the joy of seeing her friends again.

"I thought we'd never get here!" she exclaimed, gesturing dramatically as if she'd trekked for miles. "What's the news? Have I missed anything? Is Liz here? It's so good to see you!" Jenny hadn't changed and Barrie tried his best to field the torrent of questions while James extracted himself from Jenny and, in his usual way, went to help Jenny's dad unload her cases from the car boot.

James, politely, asked if Jenny's parents would like to have a cup of tea before they left, however, much to the relief of the three who were keen to catch up properly, they declined. Jenny's mother explained that the drive up from Cornwall had been very long with queues of traffic and everyone heading home from holidays on the south coast, and both she and her husband were keen to get to an inn they'd booked into in a nearby town.

After kissing Jenny goodbye, accompanied by the same pep talk the boys' fathers had given them, and very probably every parent had given their child, the earlier scenes of waving a disappearing car down the drive were repeated, this time by three children.

"Year eight already," said Jenny, picking up a case as James and Barrie each carried a bag. "Don't the year sevens look tiny? They're so young, were we that small last year?"

"I don't feel I've ever been that small, I've just always been me. Now, come on or we'll miss anything that vaguely resembles food in the dining hall."

"I'm coming, keep your hair on," said Jenny, hurriedly following James who looked back, grinning, and stuck his tongue out.

"I'm only thinking of you. Bar's nain has sent a term's worth of midnight snacks, so we're OK!"

"Hurrah for Bar's nain!" shouted Jenny, rushing to keep up with the boys. "I hope they're for all of us?"

"They are, don't worry," replied Barrie, turning into the girls' dormitory and setting the bag he was carrying by a door. "Chuck your stuff in, we'll eat now and you can unpack later."

Soon they were in the dining hall, enjoying a surprisingly good meal of roast beef and Yorkshire puddings, with sponge cake and custard for pudding.

"A good meal in your tummy is the best cure for any homesickness," the dinner lady had said kindly, piling their plates up high.

Against the background hum of children talking and eating the three exchanged news from the summer. They had met up as a four twice since their dramatic holidays at Bar's home. Once to be interviewed by the police investigating the silver theft, and the other to appear on a breakfast television show, to talk about it. Social media had gone crazy and their fifteen minutes of fame had actually been about two weeks of madness.

"We need Liz here," said Barrie, who had seen Liz as the unexpected hero of the summer

"Oh yes!"

"Absolutely," shouted Jenny and James.

"As soon as we're reunited, the four will tumble headlong into another adventure, I can feel it," said Jenny, her overactive imagination already searching for mysteries to solve or cases to crack.

"You nutter," said Barrie teasingly. "Nothing will happen just because we solved a mystery in the summer. It'll just be school as normal till Christmas."

The three finished every mouthful of their puddings and, tired from long journeys and emotional departures, they returned to their rooms, waiting till Liz could join them to first share Bar's nain's baking.

James, the tallest and oldest of the four by a few months, lay on his bed in the dark, and thought back to Jenny's assertion that there would be an adventure.

"*Bar's right,*" he thought. "*We won't have any more adventures.*"

Oh James, if only you knew how wrong you were.

Chapter Two

The New Term and a Nasty Shock

The clang of the bell the following morning heralded the start of the autumn term and, for Barrie, James and Jenny, the return of the routine of life at Grey Owls.

The three were just finishing their breakfast when, in her usual whirlwind, slightly dishevelled style, Liz joined them, throwing her bag onto the table and climbing into a chair, her right leg tucked under her. Liz was never one to sit properly if she could help it.

"Missed me?" Liz asked, grinning. It was so wonderful to see the three again, keeping in touch by phone wasn't the same. "I thought of you all together here last night and felt all alone, stuck at home. Mum wouldn't drive down for me to see you, she said there would be plenty of time to catch up this term. Parents just don't understand sometimes."

The other three agreed and James saw how Liz could feel felt a bit left out, not being a boarder, and was adamant in his mind that the four of them would always do things as a four. They were a team, the thrilling adventure in the summer had proved that.

"Year eight already," said Barrie.

"Yes, and have you seen the year sevens?" asked Liz, pointing over to two large tables in the corner where all the new pupils sat hunched over their breakfast, a few looking a bit red eyed and blotchy faced, clearly homesick. "We were never that small, they look like babies."

Liz, the youngest and smallest of the four, wasn't much older than the oldest in the new year seven group, her birthday being in August and there were a few new girls already taller than her. She was probably the most sensitive and least confident of the four, but had the purest of hearts and a fierce sense of loyalty and justice. Passionate about all animals, she had a dream of becoming a vet when she grew up, and amused the others with tales of her pets.

Jenny laughed. "I said just the same last night. They do look tiny."

Any further conversation was cut short by the ringing of a bell, summoning all the students to a whole school assembly; the normal routine for the first and last day of every term.

James, Jenny, Barrie and Liz found the year eight line and joined the end as they filed into the big assembly hall.

It was a very grand room with a polished wooden floor and wood panelling on the walls. At the front was a stage where the headmaster, Mr Pearce, sat with some of the senior teachers; the rest of the teachers sat on chairs down either side of the pupils who sat cross legged on the floor. They were arranged in year groups, with year seven at the front, going up to year eleven at the back. Grey Owls didn't have a sixth form.

"Child labour you know, using our bums to polish the floor," grinned Barrie.

"Who's that?" asked Jenny, digging Liz in the ribs and pointing across to the line of teachers flanking the pupils. Liz looked up. Level with year nine was her mum, Mrs Green the history head, who was deep in conversation with a younger woman Liz didn't recognise. The four all stared, none of them could place the stranger.

"Mum did say something about a trainee teacher," said Liz, "I guess that must be her." The four looked again at the woman with interest. She was slim, with dark brown hair tied tightly back and wore quite a pinched expression.

"She looks harsh," said Jenny, "I hope we don't have her."

"Oh, she may be OK," replied Barrie. "Probably nervous if it's her first day."

"I'm sure she'll be..." began James, but a bang from the front stage finished his thought.

The head cleared his throat and began by welcoming the students back to Grey Owls, especially those joining for the first time and how he hoped they had all enjoyed their summer break and were invigorated for a term of hard work until Christmas; the usual.

"Speaking of summer breaks," droned Mr Pearce, "it would be quite remiss of me to speak about that without mentioning the extraordinary courage, teamwork and ingenuity of four of our younger members."

To the acute embarrassment of the four the headmaster called them up onto the stage and, as they went more and more red, told the rest of the school about the adventure they had had over the summer when they had gone to stay at Barrie's home and had heard of priceless silver being stolen from a nearby stately home.

Liz, who hated attention, wished the floor would swallow her up and tried to zone out as the details of their adventures were relayed to the school. Many of the year sevens had not heard about *The Mystery of Tully Hall*, as the media had dubbed it, and sat, open mouthed, listening to the daring exploits and extreme bravery of the four. Jenny squeezed Liz's hand, bringing her back to listening.

"And I think we would all like to show our respect and pride in the actions of Jenny, James, Liz and Barrie in the customary way," boomed the headmaster, beginning to applaud. The whole school joined in. Liz fixed her eyes on her mum who was beaming with pride and pointing Liz out to the woman they now presumed was the new teacher.

Barrie looked round, red in the face and smiling out of sheer embarrassment. Even Thunder, sat up on the stage, was smiling and clapping, he noted. He wished his dad, Sarah and nain were here to see this and share in the recognition. They had all played a part, and without nain they never would have been allowed to play on the river.

James scanned the room, like Liz he felt uncomfortable with attention but was enjoying seeing everyone smiling. No. Not quite everyone, he noticed, Ryan, another year eight pupil sat stony-faced, unsmiling, his hands still and his head bowed.

"Oh well," said James to himself. "That doesn't spoil it."

The head quietened the room and the four were finally allowed to return to their places.

Miss Martin was introduced as the new staff member, a trainee teacher who would be shadowing the teachers and taking some English classes of her own. Mr Storm had been promoted to deputy head and gave the school group a stern, authoritarian look that made each pupil feel they had been noticed individually. Several other announcements were made and year duties given out. Grey Owls encouraged pride and self-discipline by having the boarders responsible for small tasks during term time such as litter picking and corridor sweeping. All the formalities over, they were all slowly filing out of assembly, heading for their forms and then the first lessons of the day. Lots of the other pupils were thumping the four on their backs and shouting congratulations, wanting more details of the summer's adventure. The four did feel like mini celebrities.

As they passed out of the hall, Liz felt a hard shove on her back, pushing her into the door frame.

"Ow!" she exclaimed as Ryan forced himself in front of her and marched off ahead.

"Hey!" shouted Barrie at the back of the disappearing brown-haired boy. "You OK, Liz?"

Liz nodded, rubbing her arm. "Pig."

"Probably left something in his room and doesn't want to be late for form and first lesson," said James, deciding not to mention that Ryan hadn't clapped with the others

"Well, he should be more careful," said Liz, as they all trudged off for a morning of maths and geography.

The morning, and indeed the rest of the day was fairly uneventful for the four. At lunch an interested group of students had joined them at their table, eager to hear more about just what exactly had gone on over the summer. Liz again went red at the mention of the part she played.

Monday turned to Tuesday and the routine of school settled once again over them all.

Jenny and Barrie's duty for the term was litter picking outside after the end of lessons each Wednesday. Depending on how much homework had been set and what the weather was doing, they would either go round together and chat as they worked, or divide the area in two and get it done twice as quickly.

James was tasked with sweeping the corridors after the end of lessons every Monday and had worked out a route to cover all the corridors as quickly as possible. Liz, being a day boarder, wasn't tasked with any chores but, as Monday was the day for the weekly staff meeting after lessons had finished, she was often left waiting for her mum to take her home and so would help James sweep. By getting it done more quickly they would then sit and do any science homework set from that afternoon's lessons. Liz was better at science than Jenny, whose skills were in English and Art, but she knew to get into vet school, she'd need top science grades, so always put extra effort into science and maths. This caused much frustration for Miss Martin, who was at pains to point out that effective written communication was needed in veterinary medicine. Liz had promised to try harder, her effort and resulting marks noticeably improving when Miss Martin set her some prose that was animal related.

The monotony of lessons, chores, tests and talk of mock exams before Christmas pushed all thoughts of the summer adventure from everyone's minds. Everyone that is until a chance overhearing by Liz upset the calm for the four.

There had not been any science homework set and, after Liz helped James sweep the corridors, he then went to help a year nine boy with his mobile phone. It was a skill James was well-known for among both pupils and staff, and he was always their first port of call if an app wouldn't work, or a phone ran out of memory, which was usually the case with Liz's phone.

Liz went to wait outside the staff room for her mum. Mrs Green was going out to listen to a talk that evening and, wanting to get away as early as possible, had instructed Liz to not go disappearing off to chat with her friends in the dorms that day, as she sometimes did when there was no homework to do.

Sitting quietly, deleting old photos from her phone to free up space, Liz heard Mr Storm's voice from inside the staff room.

"Tully Hall."

That made her prick up her ears at once. She'd only caught the two words, but what about Tully Hall? All the interest in their adventure had died down as the term had begun in earnest.

"I don't think any of them are aware, no," she heard her mum say. This was all very mysterious, aware of what?

"Probably just as well," said Mr Storm. "Now, how are the preparations for the year eight half term trip going, Keith? Is everything booked?"

Liz tuned out as Mr Atkinson gave an update on the forthcoming year eight's trip to Northumberland. In her mind, she replayed the snippets of conversation she had just overheard. Was it worth sending a message to the others about what had been said? Liz thought quickly. No, she decided, she would wait and see what her mum said on the drive home, then she could hopefully tell them more. At the moment all it would do would be to generate questions that she had no answers to.

Moving away from the staff room door, in case it was guessed she had overheard anything, Liz stood along the corridor, staring blankly at her phone, as if she were engrossed reading something on the screen. In reality she was listening hard for any clue about what the conversation had been about. Presently the door opened and she looked up. The teachers were spilling out of the staff room, much like the pupils did from lessons; keen to be off, full of hurried goodbyes. Mr Storm, passing Liz, gave her a rather rueful smile and patted her shoulder,

"Well done, Liz, well done," he said as he walked off, leaving her rather perplexed. Mr Storm was rarely anything other than intimidating, it was very odd, and well done for what? The day seemed to be getting more and more strange.

Her mum walked out, deep in conversation with Miss Martin, and smiled at her daughter. Liz and her mother were very close, and Liz had developed a love of antiques and some periods of history through her mum's passion.

Walking out to their car, Liz waited for her mum to say something about Tully Hall, expecting her to mention that it had been raised in the staff meeting. To her surprise her mum said nothing about it, instead asking how Liz's day had gone and what they'd be having for tea.

When nothing was forthcoming during the drive, Liz tried, "How was the staff meeting?" Would her mum now say the four's adventure had been spoken of?

Her mum, looking preoccupied, didn't answer immediately. "Oh, fine, the usual," she eventually responded. "Aren't the trees looking lovely at this time of year?"

Liz muttered her agreement. Clearly her mother was not going to volunteer any information about what had been discussed inside the staff room

Meeting the three as usual while they ate their breakfast cereal, Liz shared what she had heard the previous day while waiting to go home with her mum.

"There's something about Tully Hall that mum was asked if we knew about. Apparently, it's just as well we don't, or something," she began.

The other three looked puzzled and immediately, as Liz had predicted, there was a barrage of questions.

"What about the hall?" asked Barrie, sure that if there was something happening now there, his dad would have told him.

"Just as well we don't know?" repeated Jenny. "So, something about the hall is being kept secret from us?

James, deep in thought as he chewed his cornflakes slowly, looked up. "I wonder if the police case has collapsed. They do sometimes, Dad always gets so frustrated."

"It'll be on the internet if so, surely," said Jenny, getting out her phone.

Four heads crammed round the phone as Jenny put various search terms, suggested by the others, into a web page. There was nothing new.

"Not that, then. I wonder what it is?" said Barrie, instinctively wanting to find out.

"Did your mum say anything else? Anything at all?" asked James.

"No," said Liz. "Nothing at all. We went home, had a quick tea and then she went out to some talk she wanted to hear. I didn't see her till breakfast."

It was a mystery.

"See if you can find anything more out from your mum tonight," said Jenny, who, like Barrie, was desperate to find out what was going on.

"I will. I'll do my best," said Liz, as the bell rang for them all to get to form.

In the car on the way home after school, Liz again asked her mum how her day had been, hoping that she may spill the news on what was going on with Tully Hall. Barrie had sent his dad a message that day about the hall, and had received the latest photos of Sarah's restoration work in reply. It certainly seemed as if everything there was going well.

"Fine, just a normal day," replied Mrs Green. "How was yours?"

It wasn't until the next morning that a question, posed by her dad while they were having breakfast, seemed so random and out of the blue that Liz immediately thought it had to be something to do with what she'd overheard at the staff meeting.

"Do you ever look at the Grey Owls' internet page, Liz?" he asked, buttering toast.

Liz couldn't remember ever going on the Grey Owls' internet page.

"No Dad, don't think I have. Why?"

"Oh, no reason," he replied, while giving her mum a quick glance.

Her whirlwind entrance even more so than usual, Liz climbed into a chair next to the three as they hurriedly ate their breakfast, they were late that morning and the bell would be going any second.

"I think it's something to do with the Grey Owls' website," she said, explaining the odd conversation with her dad that morning, and the look he'd then given her mum.

"Can't say I've ever seen it," said Barrie, and the other two pulled faces and shook their heads, they'd not been on it either.

"I can get my laptop and we can have a look at lunch?" suggested James, as the bell rang out loudly.

"Yes, good idea, let's do that," said Liz, picking up a piece of buttery toast from Barrie's plate and biting into it

"Oi!" Barrie said, pretending to look outraged.

"I'm helping you! You don't have time to eat it all, and you hate waste," Liz replied, with a wink and an impish grin, polishing off the toast with impressive speed.

The morning's lessons of English and P.E. seemed to drag for the four. All were keen to see the website and find out what, if anything, about Tully Hall was on it, though none of them had the faintest idea about what it could be. Heading in from P.E., James nipped to his room and put his laptop into his schoolbag before meeting the others in the dining hall.

The four ate a hurried lunch of sandwiches and crisps, not wanting to waste time by queuing for the hot food. As they finished, James suggested they go to the library. It was quiet there and they would be able to browse the school's website together.

The library was wonderfully deserted. Liz headed for the booth she and James often did homework together in, and the four sat in a huddle, James bringing his laptop out and setting it up. He could have used the school's computers, but James always preferred to use his and its array of good software.

In a matter of a few moments, the school's unfamiliar external facing website appeared on the screen, recognisable from the school crest and a beautiful photograph of the school, which changed every few seconds, showing it through the seasons. The four did feel lucky to go to school in such a stunning place.

Under the News section, the four quickly spotted a relevant headline,

Four courageous young Grey Owls' pupils tackle thieves of priceless silver.

James clicked on the link and it took them to the article. Reading through it, Barrie was the first to comment. "Well, there's nothing there that we should be upset or worried about. That's a lovely write up. I shall have to send the link to Dad so he, Sarah and Nain can read it."

"Don't say it's been a wild goose chase," said Liz, sounding disheartened. "I'd really thought this morning..." her voice trailed off, as James was frowning at the screen.

"That's odd," he said, his cursor hovering over the bottom of the article. "The comments have been turned off, and the page was only updated yesterday. These comments have been turned off recently."

"I want to know what they said," said Jenny immediately, and the other two nodded in agreement. Barrie looked at James, who appeared deep in thought.

"Could you, James?"

"Probably," replied James. "If we want to see them, curiosity killed the cat and all."

"Oh, what harm can it do?" added Liz. "They're only comments."

Frowning, James' fingers flew over the keys and, after only a few minutes, old versions of the school page appeared on the screen. The four all leaned in closer to see.

Among dozens of congratulatory comments were a number of short posts dating back over three weeks.

"Losers."

"I could have done better."

"Sad losers."

"They're the sad loser," said Barrie.

"It's a troll!" said Jenny.

The four had heard of trolls, people who post upsetting comments on social media or web pages, being malicious and unkind. None of them had actually seen any troll type posts or comments before.

Reading on, the troll's attention had focused on Liz. The article had noted her feeling of under confidence in an effort to inspire others who feel that way. Instead, the troll had picked on it.

"Baby Liz, hanger on."

"Pathetic, who'd want to be with her?"

"Liability Lizzie."

Liz was visibly shocked by the comments directed at her. Jenny hugged her.

"We couldn't have managed without you."

"Absolutely," echoed the boys as James closed the lid to his laptop.

"We're a team, us four. All equal."

Liz bravely smiled, but her eyes were shining from held back tears.

"Ignore them. They're gone. Perhaps we shouldn't have even looked," said Barrie

"Whoever it is, is just jealous of you. Probably some weirdo in another country far away."

"Weirdo, yes," said James. "But whoever posted them did so from here. I checked the IP address on the troll posts.

All the same, Grey Owls'. Someone here has it in for us. The question is, who?"

Chapter Three

Upset for Liz

Liz was noticeably quieter in the days after the four had read the trolling messages. The other three were worried, and discussed how best to cheer her up after school had finished for the day and just the boarders remained.

"They're only words," said Jenny. "We have all said they don't mean anything, but I still think about how unkind they were."

"Yes," agreed James, "they have been on my mind too. I wish we hadn't seen them but, having heard there was something about Tully Hall, and then Liz's dad's question about the school website... We would only have gone mad wondering what it might have been. We had to see them." James, who hated to feel he may be at fault, was feeling responsible for Liz's upset.

Barrie guessed how James was feeling. "It's not your fault, James. You didn't write those comments. The only person who should feel ashamed is the spineless coward who wrote them."

"It's too easy for people to hide behind the internet and just say stuff without knowing or caring about the consequences," added Jenny. "Can you get any closer to seeing who wrote them?"

"No. I've tried. I can only get as far as saying that they came from Grey Owls."

"Jealousy," said Barrie. "Hopefully, now they can't put their rubbish on the page, it's the end."

"Yeah. I don't think the comments were seen by many, but if they start anything offline, we'll be ready."

Liz tried hard to put a brave face on, but she couldn't shake the image of the web page with the comments out of her mind. Was she really a loser and pathetic? She knew the other three had firmly said not, and she believed them, but even so, she felt sick to her stomach every time she thought about it.

Her mum and dad both noticed a change in Liz. "You're quiet today, Liz, are you OK?" they would ask.

"I'm fine, thanks," Liz always replied, before making an excuse about homework and escaping to her bedroom. She couldn't tell her parents about her seeing the page without risking getting James into trouble, and that was the last thing she wanted to do.

Once alone in her bedroom, the tears would flow and, however much she tried to tell herself they were just words, typed by someone who didn't matter, every comment still hurt. Liz felt terribly alone and useless.

Fortunately, it was almost as though there was a telepathic link between the four. They seemed to know how Liz was feeling and, more often than not, when sat in her room feeling miserable, her phone would vibrate with a message from one or more of the other three.

You are fab. We all love you, Jenny had sent her.

We are a team and couldn't do without you, Barrie typed, while James sent

We only work as a four. You are better than a hundred trolls. You are amazing. Believe that.

It was perhaps not surprising that, just as the comments by the troll had upset her, the comments by her friends felt like a big hug every time she read them. Slowly, over a few weeks, Liz began to feel more like her old self and, with the support of her friends, was able to put the troll's comments behind her.

The nights were beginning to draw in and Grey Owls had a brooding air to it, as if it knew winter was on the way. Lessons and school had developed a monotony, with Christmas seeming an eternity away.

Liz was fully recovered from her upset at the comments and the four discussed their upcoming adventure in two weeks' time, over lunch.

"I wonder if the kayaks will be similar to the ones we used in the summer," pondered Liz.

The four, along with a good many others from year eight were booked to go on a school trip during the October half term break. A week of outward bound activities and adventures awaited them, up in the wilds of Northumberland.

"I expect so," replied Jenny, chewing away on a piece of flapjack Barrie's nain had sent in the post. "Though we won't be as free as we were in the summer to explore, and there won't be the delicious picnics either. I wish your nain was coming Bar!" Jenny was particularly partial to the flapjacks that Barrie's nain sent with pleasing regularity.

"I spoke to her only last night, don't worry. When I said the trip was two weeks away, she promised to bake us a super tasty parcel to take."

"We must send her a thank you," said James, enjoying a chocolate brownie from Nain's latest parcel. "This is what, the second parcel already this term, and she had packed a mountain of homemade goodies with you when you came, Bar."

"Yes, good idea," said Barrie.

"Perhaps we can all club together and buy her a present to say thank you," put in Liz and the others agreed. They would look for something nice to get her in Northumberland.

"We spend one of the days on the coast and there are tourist shops. There may be something good there."

Liz knew a bit about the trip as her mother had been one of the staff members to accompany the year eight pupils the year before.

"Who was it who had that accident in his kayak?" asked Barrie.

"Matthew Waddington," replied James, remembering how it had nearly meant they were not allowed to use the kayaks in the summer. "If you look at his nose you can still just see a faint mark."

"We're kayaking pros now, no turning turtle for us." Barrie got up, brushing crumbs from his lap. "Come on, we can't be late for maths."

Jenny pulled a face, maths was not her strong point, but give her the beginnings of a tale and she had a captivating story composed in no time.

The others got to their feet and they all went to collect their bags which they had hung on pegs in a recess in the corridor.

"That's odd," said Liz, "I put mine next to yours, Jen. It's at the end now." Liz's bag had a small red dragon keyring she had bought in Wales on it.

"Probably someone knocked it off getting theirs," said Jenny, lifting her bag onto her shoulder

Liz frowned, the top zip was partly open, and she had remembered closing it tightly after English before lunch.

"What's this?" Liz exclaimed as she opened the bag to check if anything was missing and drew out a piece of squared paper that had clearly been torn from a page in an exercise book.

Written in messy block capitals were two words:

LIABILITY LIZ

Wordlessly, she held the paper out for the others to read, a feeling of dread in her stomach. James took the paper.

"Blue biro. So you just couldn't stop, could you?" he said thoughtfully. "Same phrase. You're our online troll."

Jenny put her arm round Liz. "Don't worry, shall we take it to a teacher now?"

Liz looked devastated. She had worked so hard to put the troll's comments behind her, and had genuinely felt that she'd managed it. This piece of paper however, this scrap, torn from a page in a book, scribbled on and thrust into her bag brought it all flooding back.

"I can't see how they can do anything."

"Let's meet up after lessons and discuss what to do," suggested James, taking charge and thrusting the note into his trouser pocket.

The others nodded, little knowing events would overtake them.

By the time afternoon form was over Liz was feeling terrible. Her head was pounding and she felt sick. All she wanted to do was go home and cry, she didn't feel she could face a double maths lesson.

Hanging back at the end of form she told Miss Martin, who was taking their form for that week, that she felt ill and asked if she could go and see Matron. Miss Martin looked concerned at Liz's flushed face and allowed Jenny to accompany her.

"Just drop her there. Then straight off to maths please, Jenny. Matron will look after her."

Jenny agreed, but felt awful. She knew more than anyone that what Liz needed right now was a friend with her, not to sit alone in a sick bay.

Mr Atkinson stood at the front of the class, enthusiastically explaining the finer points of basic geometry. A slim man in his late thirties, Mr Atkinson almost looked like an equation, perfectly balanced and neat. Maths was his passion and he was considered by most pupils to be a decent teacher, patient and not afraid to have some fun as long as you worked. None of the three today could concentrate, all consumed with thoughts of the note and worried about Liz.

"Are you with us Barrie?" asked Mr Atkinson, pointedly. The class was silent

"Sorry, sir. Pardon?" said Barrie, jolted back into the room and going rather crimson.

"Page 47 in your textbook questions one to six, please," repeated Mr Atkinson and Barrie hurriedly began to thumb through the pages.

It was as his head was bent, looking for the page number, that he caught sight of something out of the corner of his sharp eyes that made him stop in his tracks.

A torn page in a squared paper exercise book.

Quick as a striking snake Barrie lunged across the desks and seized the book, snatching it out of Ryan's hands and causing him to give a cry of outrage.

"Hey! Give that back!

Ryan made a grab for his book but Barrie held him back, passing the book to James.

"Torn page."

"Stop all this!" shouted Mr Atkinson, striding quickly over and separating Barrie and Ryan. "Now what is all this about?"

Barrie, out of breath in the sudden excitement, looked across desperately at James who was drawing the scrap of paper from his trouser pocket and offering it to the torn page. It fitted perfectly.

"Well, sir," began James, "a nasty note was put in Liz Green's bag at lunchtime and Bar has noticed it's come from

Ryan's book, look." James held up the book and torn section. "And that's not all."

"I...I..." Ryan spluttered, eyes blazing and his face almost purple with rage.

"Silence. I don't want to hear it. I think you three boys and I had better go immediately and see the headmaster."

The three were propelled swiftly along the top corridor towards the headmaster's office. The corridor was beautifully panelled and even more daunting than the rest of the school. Miss Martin was writing a lesson plan in a nearby room and was asked by Mr Atkinson, in a very formal manner, if she could please go and supervise his year eight maths class. She went at once, sensing from his tone the seriousness of the situation.

Mr Atkinson knocked on the open door to the deputy head's office, which now belonged to Mr Storm, and poked his head inside. It was empty. He instructed Ryan to wait in there and closed the door behind him.

Mr Atkinson then knocked on the door to the head's office. "Headmaster. Mr Pearce." read the brass plaque on the door. He went through the door, closing it firmly behind him and there was the sound of hushed voices from inside the office.

James and Barrie, standing in silence outside the office, were summoned inside to give their account. James explained that he had noticed the comments on the school website.

"You must view it very frequently," said the head. "Those comments were removed almost at once and then when they continued, all comments were removed and the function locked." James didn't answer, he didn't want to get into trouble for being able to access old versions, and anyway, Ryan was the one who has caused all the upset here, the focus, thought James, should be on him. The head mistook James' silence for embarrassment at reading a story about himself repeatedly.

"Well, well done both of you, quite the detectives," said the head. "Return to your class and I shall speak to Ryan."

Returning to class, the boys discreetly updated Jenny who was desperate to share the news with Liz.

"She looked so wretched when I left her with Matron," said Jenny. "This will, I'm sure, make her feel better. Ryan has been found out, he'll be in trouble and the nastiness will be stopped."

After maths Jenny raced to the sick bay to see Liz before science and told her all about Barrie's discovery and Ryan being hauled up in front of the headmaster.

"But why has he done it?" asked Liz, "and why pick on me? I've never done anything to him, none of us have."

"I don't know," said Jenny, "and I don't think they can make him tell us why. At least everyone knows now, and so it won't continue. Are you coming to science?"

Liz didn't feel up to lessons and so stayed with Matron until her mum came for her after the end of lessons. Hugging her tightly, her mum promised her a special tea that night. She had heard how the children had known about the article comments, as well as the note, and now realised why Liz had been so quiet.

The other three didn't see Ryan for the rest of the day. They were all shocked that he seemed to have been behind everything.

"He was a bit moody at the start of term," recalled James, "but he's been OK since, quiet perhaps."

"I'd not really noticed him," said Barrie.

Liz heard that night that the headmaster had spoken to Ryan's parents and Ryan would be apologising to the four the following day. He would also be in detention for two weeks. She sent an update to the other three via their group chat on their phones.

The next day brought worse news. After a muttered apology from Ryan, where he didn't make eye contact with any of them, Liz was not feeling any happier and was even more upset to learn that her mum would not be joining them on the half term trip. Miss Martin would be going instead, to get experience of a residential trip. The four all really liked Mrs Green, and had enjoyed many teas and weekend days at Liz's home. They were not so sure about Miss Martin. She was very "cardboard" as Barrie had described her.

"Ryan won't be coming though," said James, "so it'll be OK, Liz."

Liz nodded and smiled. That would at least be something.

As bad turned to worse, a terrible shock awaited them the following day. Ryan, provided he behaved well to half term, was to be allowed to go on the trip.

Liz, clearly still affected, told the others over breakfast. They couldn't believe it.

"But after all that?" questioned Jenny. "It's mad."

"I don't want to go," said Liz, tears suddenly welling up. "I'm not going to go."

Jenny put her arms round her. "If you're not, I'm not," she said.

"Nor us," added James and Barrie together.

"We stick together, just like in the summer," James added, though he had been badly looking forward to the trip.

Unless they could change the mind of determined Liz, it looked like the Northumberland adventure would be over before it had even begun.

Chapter Four

Northumberland or Not?

The next week was very strained for the four. Ryan, obviously keen to go on the school trip, behaved very properly, albeit stiffly towards Liz, Jenny Barrie and James.

"Let me get the door for you, Liz," he would say, but there was no smile, no friendship, no feeling of genuine remorse for his behaviour. He did have appointments during school hours with a lady who came in. None of the four knew her.

"Probably because of the bullying," said James. "Dad says there are lots of intervention schemes set up for kids who start going off the rails."

Barrie, James and Jenny didn't mention the half term trip once to Liz that week, not wanting her to confirm that she didn't want to go and hoping the situation with Ryan would improve.

"What shall we do if Liz won't go on the trip?" asked Barrie, over dinner one evening when the three were sitting together. "I guess I could ask Dad if we could all come back to mine."

"We can't do that," said James. "It was very good of him to take us all for the week in summer, we can't impose on him and Sarah again."

"I'm sure he wouldn't mind," replied Barrie, desperate to have a fun option where the four could stay together, "and Nain I'm sure would love to see you all."

"Well, my house is out," said James. "There isn't really room for three guests and with dad's shifts we would have to be as quiet as mice much of the time while he is sleeping." James' father was a police officer and had taught James many tricks and tips to look out for, which James enjoyed sharing with the other three. They all now knew the phonetic alphabet and what the police codes were.

"Are you twelve?" was a particularly useful one when one of them phoned another and wanted to know if anyone could hear them.

"We could I guess go to mine, though I'd been working on mum to let us stay there in the summer," said Jenny. "Cornwall is much nicer in the summer. It's beautiful all year, but we could do much more in July, perhaps even camp out."

James and Barrie were both keen to camp in Cornwall in the summer and didn't want to overstay their welcome with Jenny's family too early.

"So, it's really a choice of Northumberland outward bounds or we all go home. Oh, I do hope Liz comes round," said Barrie, looking as glum as the other two were feeling.

"I'm sure she will," said James. "Give her another week. I don't think Ryan will dare say anything to upset her. He seemed desperate to go on the trip rather than go home."

Thankfully as the weeks went on, life at Grey Owls returned very much to normal. Ryan drifted back to being just another pupil to the four, there were no more comments or notes and, fuelled by Nain's delicious baking, they worked hard for the end of half term tests.

Liz had quite got over her anxiety about the trip and the four eagerly planned what they would try and do.

"Miss Martin and Mr Atkinson seem OK. I think Miss Martin could be quite fun away from school, she is young after all."

Liz looked at Barrie. "Still would have been better with mum."

The others agreed.

"Nain has sent me a message to say she's posted us a bumper parcel of midnight snack food. She thought we may work up an appetite with all the activities, so she packed extra."

"Oh, that is a point. We sleep in dorms in bunk beds, Mum said," said Liz. "One for the girls and one for the boys. It may be difficult to have midnight feasts."

"Don't worry," said Jenny. "We'll sort something, I can always come up with a weird and wonderful tale to get rid of the teachers for a bit."

"You and your stories, Jen," said James. "You are so good."

Jenny smiled, writing was her absolute passion.

The Saturday before the half term holiday, Jenny, James and Barrie were greeted at nine o'clock in the morning by Mrs Green, with a grinning Liz in the front seat of the small blue car. All the students going on the trip, and their parents, had received a letter detailing all the kit they would need to take. It was mostly what the boarders had already, things like warm clothes, a waterproof coat, towel, shoes for indoor wear, sturdy walking boots or shoes. In amongst the list were items that caused the four to wonder just what they'd be doing on the trip. Shoes, in addition to the indoor and walking, that would tolerate being submerged in water.

Leggings and long-sleeved vest top or similar for wearing under a wetsuit. They all felt excited reading that.

Mrs Green had kindly offered to take the four into the nearest town that day so they could buy anything they needed from the list that they didn't already have and so picked them up in her car with Liz. The four all needed some items; Liz just needed some boots. She already had a pair but they were now a bit too tight and well worn. James and Barrie both needed some leggings, while Jenny didn't have any rough shoes to be submerged.

"I'm sure you don't want me hanging about you," Mrs Green said, as she pulled into a space in a car park. "I'll come with you to get the footwear sorted. Jenny, did you say you needed some too?"

"Yes, Mrs G. Underwater ones."

"Right, we can get those and Liz's boots at a shop just round the corner. Then, if you'd like to meet me back here for midday, I thought you might all enjoy a treat of a pizza lunch." Mrs Green had long since given up on trying to get the children to call her by her first name, Susan, when out of school. Mrs G was the least formal the children would use.

There was an enthusiastic chorus of agreement from the four. They all considered pizza to be one of the best meals out ever and all grinned widely.

The five of them all walked to the shoe shop where Liz and Jenny tried on boots. Liz tried on a smart pair of walking boots, black and grey with pink flashes, and felt very proud of them. She was sure they'd be up for anything. Jenny wasn't sure what she'd need, so Mrs Green guided her to a practical, lightweight walking shoe that wouldn't absorb too much water and get heavy.

After the two pairs were bought, Mrs Green said she'd take them back to the car and, to give the children more time, would meet them at Andrea's pizzeria at one pm. That would give them a good three hours to wander round town and get whatever else they felt they needed.

"We'll get those legging things first," said James, wanting to get the essentials out of the way. "Lead on Liz."

Liz knew where to go and within twenty minutes both boys had bought the right clothes to wear under wetsuits.

"Batteries," suggested Barrie.

"Batteries? What for?" asked Jenny, looking confused and getting out her kit list to check.

"Our torches. We will be taking them won't we? Might need them if we are out at night, so we must make sure they won't run out when we need them."

"We won't be out at night," said Liz. "They used to do a night-time woodland walk, but three or four years ago one of the boys thought it would be a good laugh to sneak off. They almost had a search party called out to find him. Mum said they stopped doing the night walk after that."

"If we find a mystery though," persisted Barrie, "we might need them."

The other three laughed, they knew how Barrie felt, and were all keen for an adventure.

"Yes, in case we find a mystery," agreed James, winking at the girls.

The four had all bought torches in the summer, which for the three boarders had proved invaluable for feasts and meet ups after lights out. The room lights were too obvious, shining out through the glass panel above the door.

Batteries purchased, they all enjoyed spending a few hours mooching around the shops. It was just nice to be on their own, away from school for a bit.

Andrea's lived up to their expectations. A small, authentic Italian restaurant it made the thinnest, tastiest pizzas the children had ever enjoyed. They could see them being baked on a hot stone and loved the accents of the staff, who were all Italian. Salvatore, their waiter, seemed genuinely delighted to see them and replied "Grazie", the Italian word for thank you, with a beaming smile after each selection from the menu.

"He's like pure sunshine," said Jenny, "I can't help but smile back."

"I'd like to go to Italy," said James, basing his desire purely on that meal. The other three nodded.

Mrs Green had been before and encouraged them. She really liked the four, they were easy company. She had been very impressed with their handling of the note incident and grateful how they had banded round Liz. Mrs Green still had friends she'd made at school and knew these four would always stay in contact.

"It's beautiful. I went with university friends and we stayed up in the mountains in southern Italy. It was so unspoilt and relaxed, a slower pace of life. You four should go as a group when you're old enough to travel alone, you would love it."

The four looked at each other. Yes, that sounded like an amazing thing to do in the future.

Thanking Mrs Green effusively for their trip into town and lunch, the three almost rolled out of the car back at Grey Owls, they were so full of pizza and gelato, Italian ice cream.

They went to their rooms to add their purchases to their bags and check, and recheck, that they had packed everything they needed. Monday morning would soon be here.

Monday morning of half term felt different at Grey Owls. Most of the boarders had returned home for the holidays and only a few, and those going on the trip, remained.

After an early morning breakfast, the school minibus drew round to the front entrance of the school. It was navy blue and had the school's name, crest and a rather mournful looking grey owl painted on it.

Mr Atkinson was at the wheel, while Miss Martin called, cajoled and corralled the twelve excited children onto the bus.

Mrs Green had arrived with Liz that morning and stayed to see them off. She had passed Liz a bag as she got on the bus and, as the four found seats close to each other, Liz opened the bag.

"Oh, Mum is fab!" she exclaimed, feeling a pang of sadness that she wasn't coming with them. "Look, she's given each of us a packet of our favourite sweets just like she did when we set off to yours in the summer, Bar."

Liz handed the three packets out. To James, she gave Yorkshire Mixture, Barrie, chocolate covered raisins, and Jenny pear drops. Fizzy cola bottles she opened herself.

Waving madly at Mrs Green, their cheeks bulging with sweets, the four settled themselves as the bus pulled, or rather lurched, away down the drive. Normally Mr Merryweather drove it, Mr Atkinson wasn't quite as familiar with the old vehicle as he caused the gearbox to scream while he fought for second gear.

"We'll be lucky to get there," said Jenny, wincing as the bus jolted into third.

"I'm sure there's a gear in there somewhere Mr Atkinson!" shouted Miss Martin, laughing.

"I've just not found one I like yet!" shouted back Mr Atkinson, laughing as the minibus juddered to a stop at the end of the drive.

The Yorkshire Dales rolled by as the children all looked out of the windows, contentedly sucking or chewing their sweets.

They stopped for an early packed lunch not far from the outward bounds centre where they were going to stay, stretching their legs in a small car park, with picnic benches at one end overlooking a large green open space.

The cook at Grey Owls had made paper bag pack ups for each person, each containing a sandwich, packet of crisps, yoghurt and piece of fruit and there was quite a time spent swapping between each other as everyone tried to trade for their favourite flavours.

"I think this will be the last decent meal we get if Mr Atkinson is in charge of the food," said Liz, the other three looked at her, glancing to see Mr Atkinson was out of earshot. "Mum said his sandwich combinations are erm, questionable to say the least."

"What like?" asked Jenny. "How wrong can you honestly go with a sandwich?"

"According to Mum, very!" replied Liz. "He is very fond of things like jam and chocolate spread and peanut butter and all those sorts of things."

"Sounds OK," replied Jenny.

"Yeah, but not when you mix them all together," retorted Liz, and Jenny pulled a face.

"It's a good job we have so much baking from Nain, then," said Barrie, "it sounds like we might need it. My bag is full of her brownies and flapjacks." They all agreed, tucking into their lunch hungrily, and hoping Miss Martin might prove a better cook.

"We will be straight into activities when we get there, so your food needs to have time to settle," explained Mr Atkinson, a veteran of these trips. "Barrie, must you glug down quite so much water? You are not a camel you know, and we won't be stopping till we get there."

Barrie blushed and a snigger could be heard from Ryan. James shot him a furious look. He was not going to let Ryan, or anyone, spoil what promised to be a fun week.

Sandwiches eaten, the bus again lurched into motion and soon they passed the county sign for Northumberland.

"The land of castles," breathed Jenny, already dreaming up a story in her mind, of damsels in distress locked in castle towers and heroic knights on majestic horses doing battles and brave deeds to rescue them.

Liz was thinking of all her mum had said would be in store: rock climbing, abseiling, kayaking, archery, orienteering. She wiggled her toes in her boots, her socks were thick and her new walking boots sturdy. She felt ready for anything and couldn't wait to get back on the water in a kayak.

James and Barrie were doing something on their phones, James showing some app or other, Liz looked at them, engrossed, and for the thousandth time felt so lucky to have such friends. The start of the term had not been a great time for her, but they had banded together and shown the power of true friendship. Smiling, she rested her head back and closed her eyes.

Heavy braking and a violent swing to the left signalled the arrival at the youth hostel which would be home for the rest of the week. The minibus bounced down a stone track before rounding a bend and coming to a shuddering stop in front of a low-roofed converted barn that instantly reminded the four of Barrie's nain's home.

Two men in their twenties appeared from the building, smiling as everyone piled out of the minibus.

Miss Martin had been right about Barrie not being a camel, and pointed him towards the entrance where he disappeared inside to find a toilet.

Everyone else meanwhile gathered round the two men as they introduced themselves. "We are your instructors for the week and will make sure that you stay safe but have an amazing time," said the slightly shorter, brown-haired one, clapping his hands. "I'm Morton and this is David," he continued, pointing to his friend who was a good bit taller than him, with more gingery hair. "First things first, put all your phones and valuables into your bags and stow them in the lounge in the hostel, first door on your right through the entrance. We will get straight off to make the most of the daylight."

James grabbed Barrie's bag as well as his own and as Barrie returned, all the bags were in and they were gathered round Morton and David for their first briefing. Barrie's phone, of course, was still in his coat pocket.

Chapter Five

Flittermouse Cliffs

"We need you in groups of six," Miss Martin said as she divided them up. Annoyingly for the four, she didn't put them together in one group. Barrie and Liz were together, Jenny and James in the other.

"Right. You lot are with David and myself," continued Morton, pointing to the group Barrie and Liz were in, "and you others, are going to join Pete and Phil over the bridge for an afternoon of archery. See if you are as skilled with bows and arrows as people of yesteryear. Mr Atkinson, do you remember the way from last year?"

Mr Atkinson nodded, smiling and the six with him set off down a path.

"OK, now we need to get you kitted up. We have a bit of a walk and then there are some fabulous cliffs to climb up and abseil down." Morton pointed towards a pile of ropes, harnesses and hard hats. There was excited chatter among the six; this sounded like great fun. Liz and Barrie grinned at each other, looking forward to a good scramble.

Soon they were all adorned in harnesses and helmets, all brightly coloured in blues, oranges and greens. David and Morton had checked the fit as each child found suitable kit for their size and David now swung a huge length of orange rope across his shoulders. Miss Martin, claiming to be ready for anything and up for everything, was also kitted up and smiled round at everyone.

"Off we go then," announced Morton who had a large coil of blue rope across his shoulders as well as a red and grey rucksack on his back. "I'll lead off and David will bring up the rear, it's about a mile and a half, so if anyone needs a rest, do shout up."

They set off in the opposite direction to the other group, up a track away from the hostel.

Water could be heard and soon, passing through a narrow wooden gate, their path followed the side of a narrow river, dotted with large rocks, so that the water tumbled over them and swirled around as it found its own path.

"This is the gorge," said David, from the rear of the group, "we've some gorge walking planned for later in the week."

"Gorge walking?" asked Liz. "Not walking in it?"

"Yes!" laughed David. "You'll love it."

Liz and Barrie exchanged glances of uncertainty, it looked cold!

The path led on. Trees to the right, looking magnificent in their autumn colours, grew on a bank that sloped upwards, giving way at the top to grey rocky outcrops where smaller, stunted trees appeared to cling on. The gorge to the left got slowly narrower and deeper. As if a giant had once hand carved it with a chisel from the rocks, Liz thought.

"We couldn't kayak down that," said Barrie to Liz. "It's not at all like by Tully Hall."

The rocky gorge had a dramatic feel to it. Unlike the calm, wide, open river the four had adventured on in the summer, beyond the banks high cliffs now bordered the gorge on both sides. Green ferns grew in crevices and, on any small cleft in the rocks, small bare trees stood as if clinging tightly to the cliff. High above all round, there was an orange quality to the light, as the low autumn sun reflected off the foliage of trees growing higher up, their leaves already a picture of golds, oranges, greens, and reds.

"Jenny will love this," said Liz. "Her descriptive mind would be on overdrive, just look at the colours."

Barrie agreed.

The path they were on left the gorge, and they scrambled up a steep section in woodland, before it returned back down and again followed the water. It had widened out considerably with the base of the cliff now about 15 metres from the side of the gorge. Morton stopped, dropping the rucksack from his back and the rope from his shoulders.

"Welcome!" he announced in a dramatic voice. "Welcome to Flittermouse Cliffs!"

Miss Martin and all the children stared up in awe. Towering above them was an immense rock face. Jagged and imposing, it looked to Liz like the giant had, after carving out the gorge, hacked roughly at the cliff face, leaving overhangs and narrow ledges, sheer faces and crevices. The same thought went through everyone's mind - How on earth would they ever climb that?

"Why is it called Flittermouse Cliffs?" asked Barrie, who always liked knowing these types of things; like Tully Hall, the children's abbreviation for the Welsh word Tylluan meaning owl. "Does flittermouse mean something?"

"It does," said Morton, nodding. "It means bat. These cliffs were once home to a huge bat colony. Apparently, there were so many that as dusk approached and they all flew out, the sky turned quite dark because of them all, and flittermouse is the old English word for bat."

"Flittermouse," repeated Liz. "It's a far nicer word for bats than bat! They sound quite cute, being a mouse that flitters."

"You'd cuddle any animal," teased Barrie, grinning.

"Are there any bats there now?" asked Miss Martin.

"Some, yes, but not on the same scale," replied Morton. "They live in cracks and crevices like those," he pointed up and they all followed his gaze.

"Right, shall we do some climbing?" asked David, who had taken off his coat and was rigged up in harness and helmet, with a rope attached to the front of his harness and lots of shaped metal clips hanging from the back of it.

Taking a harness out of the bag, Morton stepped into it and fastened it securely around his waist. He then tied the other end of the orange rope that David had fastened to his harness, to his own harness, connecting it to a small device which he explained was called a belay.

David pointed up the rock face. "Can you see the path of bolts?" he asked, and moved his arm to show the line of shiny bolts fastened securely at intervals up the cliff. "I will climb up following those bolts, clipping a quick-draw onto each one as I go." He held out a pair of the large clips, which he informed them were called carabiners, joined together by a short length of cord, called a sling. "Morton will belay me up, so if I slip, I don't fall, and then it will be your turn." Mixed feelings of excitement and fear ran through the six children. It was so steep!

Morton had fed most of the rope through his belay, so that the distance of rope connecting him to David was short. Miss Martin and the six children watched as David, looking up at the path he would follow, took his first step up Flittermouse Cliff as Morton let out the line, keeping it quite straight. From a pouch on his harness, David kept dusting his hands with what Morton explained was chalk, leaving white powdery handprints up the cliff face. At the first bolt, David paused, unclipped a quick-draw from the back of his harness, and fastened it to the bolt, connecting the other end of it to his rope, so the rope now went from him, through the carabiner and then down to Morton.

"Now I'm totally safe," he called down and, as the children gasped in horror, he let go of the rock completely.

David dropped only a few feet before the rope between him and Morton went taut, and he was suspended by the quick-draw, hanging quite happily waving down at them.

"See, if you slip, do not panic, do not worry, you are attached by the rope and we will not let you fall," shouted down David, regaining his footing and resuming his climb.

Morton looked at the children. Emily, a quiet girl with long brown hair and big brown eyes still looked worried.

"You'll be roped from above," said Morton to her, smiling. "So, if you slip, you won't even fall a foot."

Morton continued letting out the rope as David steadily climbed higher.

"He makes it look so easy," said Barrie, feeling a bit in awe at David's skill.

"Heavens to Betsy," murmured Liz in agreement.

David got to the top and signalled to Morton that he was ready for the first of the group to climb up.

"The next climber is the seconder," explained Morton. "As you climb, you need to unclip all the quick-draws that David put in, and clip them to the back of your harness. Who is up for that?"

Miss Martin was very keen to impress the year eights and so immediately stepped forward, volunteering. Morton unfastened the rope from his harness, and tied it securely to Miss Martin's. Accompanied by shouts of encouragement from the six children she began to climb steadily, removing the quick-draws as she went. About half way up, she faltered, unable to see where was suitable to put her hand.

"Look for the chalk," shouted up Morton, and, spotting a dusty patch just to the left of where she had been trying, Miss Martin reached out for it and continued.

Morton explained to the six, "The chalk is there to aid David's grip as he climbs. It isn't strictly necessary on this climb, but we found that the marks it leaves can be really useful when people can't see where to reach for." It was a clever idea, thought Barrie.

Miss Martin reached the top safely. There were rowdy cheers from below and excited clapping.

"Rope below!" shouted David, and the orange rope was let back down the cliff face.

"Who's going to be the next to climb then?" asked Morton. Seeing that Emily looked nervous still, and knowing she'd only get more so, he quickly gestured to Emily to come forwards and she shyly stood as he fastened the rope to her harness, checked that all the straps on it were tight, and that her helmet was fastened and comfortable.

"Right Emily, reach for the sky and be the star that you are," he said, followed more loudly by, "Three cheers for Emily."

The other five cheered and yelled encouragement and, a little tentatively, Emily began to climb. About a third of the way up was a slight overhang. Emily reached up, taking most of her weight in her arms, when the one foot she had still in contact with the rock suddenly slipped. She let out a scream of fright as she lost her hand hold and the five children below gasped, but David had a firm hold of the taut rope and, although she bumped her side against the face of the overhang, she didn't drop more than a few inches.

"It's OK!" Morton called up to her. "Are you alright? Just take a minute and carry on when you're ready, David has you."

Emily shouted back down that she was not hurt, and grabbed hold of the rock more confidently, pulling herself up valiantly.

"I hope she didn't damage her phone," said Barrie, to Liz, thinking about his new phone in his coat pocket.

"All our phones are back at the hostel in our bags, probably for that reason," said Liz. "Didn't you hear Morton?"

"Oh rats, must have been when I went inside at the start," said Barrie.

Ryan, overhearing, couldn't resist making a wise comment, "Be funny if you broke it"

"Shut up, Ryan," said Barrie, wondering what to do.

Emily was making great time up the top section of the cliff and the group at the bottom cheered wildly as she made it to the top and stood proudly. Even at that distance, they could see her smile as wide as that of a Cheshire cat.

As Emily was being untied at the top, he went to Morton and explained. Morton was fine about it and had an easy solution.

"Pop it in the top pocket of my bag and it will be quite safe," he said. "Are you going up next?" Barrie did. The climb was amazing. Reaching and finding holds for hands and feet, transferring weight across and navigating the best path up was great fun, though Barrie thought he would feel very differently if it wasn't for the safety gear he knew was keeping him safe.

Liz went next, pausing at any crevice to listen for bats, or flittermice as she knew she would always now call them.

Another half hour later and everyone was at the top, Morton being the last up.

David and Morton congratulated them all, declaring it a "First class climb."

"You've done all the hard work. Now it's the fun part, abseiling down. We want a nice controlled descent, no throwing yourself down at breakneck speed. We're just going a slight bit further on to have the best descent," said David, as Morton coiled up the long orange rope. He'd brought the rucksack up with him on his back, but had left the blue rope below.

"It's just a spare, we're not going far and will pick it up on the way back," he explained, when sharp eyed Liz had spotted its absence, and headed off to the abseiling point with the rest following.

About 50 metres further along the cliff, they stopped. From his bag Morton produced a number of metal objects he called descenders and David secured the rope around the trunk of a huge old tree growing next to the cliff top path. Showing the group how the device would enable them to descend at their own pace, Morton fastened himself to the rope and backed towards the edge of the cliff.

"Stepping off is the hardest bit, but try and keep your body upright, and enjoy the journey down," he slowly disappeared over the edge, showing them how easy it was to control the speed.

Miss Martin volunteered to go next and tentatively lowered herself over the edge with a few squeaks of fright.

Emily and Liz followed, there were whoops of delight and applause from the bottom as each reached there safely.

Barrie then began his descent, determined to make a good job of it, and impress David and Morton. There were rock faces near his home, Pen y Bryn. If he could learn how to do this, he could have hours of fun exploring in the holidays.

It was on this steady, controlled descent that Barrie spotted some bolts in the cliff face going off to his left. They were dull, and he called down to Morton, pointing to them.

"Old path," called back Morton, "not been used for ages now, goes too close to a bat colony that moved in."

Barrie followed the bolts with his eyes and saw how they passed above a silver birch tree that was somehow managing to grow on the narrowest of ledges and then on to a horizontal crevice, about four feet wide and only six inches high.

"Come on, we've a campfire to make," called up Morton.

"Sorry, coming," said Barrie, giving the path of bolts a final glance. His sharp eyes suddenly noticed something out of place. A carabiner was clipped to a bolt near the crevice, as if someone had forgotten to remove it while climbing. It was a different type to the ones they were using, but it was definitely one.

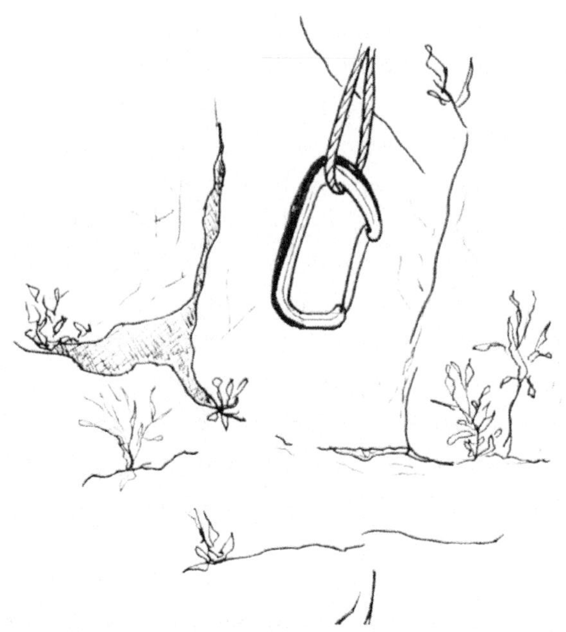

As he continued down, Barrie asked himself why it looked so out of place. Nearing the bottom it struck him, of course, it was shiny. That meant it was recent!

Looking back up at it after he was safely down and unclipped, Barrie noticed how the silver birch leaves almost completely hid the carabiner. Morton, he noticed, when he wasn't taking photos as each person abseiled, kept also glancing up at that section. It was about 20 metres off the abseil line, and Barrie felt sure there was something amiss.

Pretending he had not heard Morton, he asked again about the path of bolts.

"They've not been used this year since the bats moved in. It's illegal to disturb bat roosts. I noticed they were in when I climbed before the season began, so set up the other route that we've all climbed instead. It's a better route to be honest, I don't think we'll come back to this one."

Barrie continued musing as the others, and finally David, descended.

"Excellent work everybody. That's been a really good afternoon's climb," said Morton.

David, who was grinning as he coiled up the orange rope added, "Back, get washed up, sort your kit out and then how about a campfire?"

A raucous cheer of agreement echoed round the gorge and up the cliffs, with everyone feeling exhilarated after their abseil.

"You've been here too long, gone bats!" laughed Morton.

"Gone flittermouse, you mean?" replied Miss Martin, making everyone laugh more.

Happy at their climbing achievement, they all started back along the path that would take them past where they'd climbed and back to the hostel.

During the walk, Barrie managed a hushed conversation with Liz. Why be so adamant a path was not in use, when it evidently had been, and recently too?

Liz was sceptical. "Anyone could have left it there, but we'll discuss it with the others," she said, and Barrie agreed.

"It's probably nothing," he admitted, reflecting that it was just one carabiner. But all the way back he just couldn't shake the feeling that something was going on.

Chapter Six

Barrie's Phone

The sun was beginning to set by the time Barrie, Liz and the rest of the rock climbing group arrived back at the hostel. Their pace had slowed on the return, happy but worn out by the excitement, the long bus trip and the effort of climbing. Jenny was waving at them from inside the hostel and ran out to meet her friends.

"I've bagged a bunk together by the window Liz, do you want to be top or bottom?"

"Erm, I don't mind, you choose," replied Liz, unstrapping her helmet and unbuckling her harness. "How was your afternoon?"

"It was really good," said Jenny. "The bows were pretty tough, my arms are aching but I'm a hot shot with a bow and arrow, I hit a gold! What did you get up to?"

"We walked up a path along the gorge, scrambled through some steep woods and ended by some huge cliffs. They were massive and used to be home to thousands and thousands of bats. Flittermouse Cliffs they're called, because that is an old word for bat."

"Oh, like coney is for rabbit?" asked Jenny, interrupting. Liz looked confused.

Miss Martin, overhearing, nodded. "Well done, Jenny, that's right. Coney is an old English word for rabbits, and brock is for?" she paused

"Oh, I know this," said Jenny, screwing her eyes shut as she tried to remember. "Badger!"

"Top marks!" smiled Miss Martin. "Now, perhaps you can continue this catch up inside while you unpack and wash?"

"Yes, miss," replied Jenny and Liz in unison, and followed the rest of the group inside.

The hostel was a single storey, stone-built barn and had immediately reminded all of the four of Barrie's nain's home. Barrie made a mental note to ask Morton or David if it had once been a cow byre, as Nain's home had. A protruding porch was well equipped with stiff brushes and scrapers for dealing with muddy boots. Liz stamped her boots on the mat, before unlacing them and adding them to the pile. They didn't look new now, she thought, wishing they still were as clean and smart as they'd been that morning.

Through the entrance there was a door immediately to the right, which led to the lounge area where the children had stowed their bags on first arriving. A small kitchen could be seen straight ahead from the entrance and a door to the left was entitled "Girls' Dorm".

Jenny pushed open the door while pointing in the opposite direction, down a corridor, saying, "The boys' dorm is at the other end of the building at the end of the corridor and the teachers' dorm is on the left of the corridor first. We have a toilet and shower in our dorm, so do the boys."

Going into the dorm, Liz saw six sets of bunk beds. There were three other girls on the trip, Emily, Rachel and Sky, who were busy unpacking their bags.

Jenny took Liz to their bunk. "I'll go on the bottom then," she said, and passed Liz's bag to her.

They both unpacked their things and queued up to wash in the sink.

"There are more showers and toilets in the wooden hut just to the left of the hostel, but it's getting dark now, I'm happy to wait in line," explained Jenny who had had a chance to explore after the archery. "Morton and David have beds and stuff at the other end of the wooden hut, Pete told us today. He and Phil live close by and just come on days when they are needed.

Across in the boys' dorm, James and Barrie were having similar conversations. James filled Barrie in on the afternoon's archery and his belief that modern soldiers must be relieved they don't have to fight in that way.

Barrie then began to tell James about his afternoon's climbing, eager to share his gut feeling that there was something not quite right.

"I was abseiling down and about two thirds of the way down, I saw some old bolts in the cliff face, similar to those we'd used to climb up. Morton said it was a climbing path they used to use but that they didn't now, as a colony of bats had moved into a nearby crevice."

"What's odd about that?" asked James, "I would imagine you can't easily get the bolts out of the cliff, so would just leave them in."

"It wasn't that," said Barrie, pausing while another pupil, Tim, came from the bathroom and passed by. "Along the path, beyond a silver birch tree, near to the crevice where the bats are, was a carabiner, just like those we were clipping to the bolts." Again, he paused as Mr Atkinson poked his head in at the dorm door, and said that dinner would be in the lounge in five minutes.

"Left there by someone from when it was last used?" asked James, who had a useful trait of always trying to find a logical explanation.

"I don't think so," said Barrie, scrubbing his hands in the sink. Drying them, he continued. "Not last year anyway. The carabiner was bright and shiny. It looked brand new and clean."

James shrugged, "Perhaps someone who didn't know about the bats climbed? I take it anyone can access the cliffs?"

"I guess," said Barrie, a little disheartened, "I'd not thought of that. I just got to the bottom and Morton kept glancing back up at the bolts and bat roost. It was well away from the abseil line."

"Hmm, I can't see it being a super mystery," said James, who shared Barrie's feeling that, since their exciting adventure in the summer, normal life was a little bit dull, and so any potential mystery was quickly seized upon.

A shout of "Dinner!" stopped any further conversation and they joined everyone in the lounge which doubled up as a dining room. Sitting with Liz and Jenny, they enjoyed generous bowls of spaghetti Bolognese.

Looking round, Liz noticed neither Morton nor David was there. "Are they not eating with us, Miss?" she asked.

Miss Martin shook her head. "No. They have their meals in peace in their hut, and tonight I believe they are building us a little campfire to enjoy."

"I wish I'd brought some marshmallows," said Rachel.

Mr Atkinson, to everyone's delight, produced a bag from next to him. "Not my first time." He grinned, and they all smiled back

"So, tell us more about your day", said Liz, who was looking forward to trying archery later in the week.

"You'll love it, Liz. Phil started off with the history of archery, somewhere in South Africa, I think. In Britain it was a mediaeval weapon for battle and hunting, defending castles and the like by firing arrows through the slits in their walls. Phil said the range of the shortbow was about one hundred yards, so he and Pete set the targets at forty, seventy and one hundred yards. 'Old money,' Phil said, not metres, but I don't think there is much difference."

"It's really weird," James added. "Mine kept hitting the ground to start with. You have to aim higher than where you want it to go and hope that as it arches up and drops down it hits your target. All physics stuff we did a few weeks ago, really. I can't believe the native Indians managed to fire them accurately while galloping about bareback on horses."

"I got a gold. Hit the middle of the target at seventy yards," Jenny said proudly.

"I didn't get closer than a blue," said James, shutting his eyes as he recalled the colour sequence. "It goes white, black, blue, red and gold."

"Then we had a go at the longbow," continued Jenny. "That was as tall as me! It was really hard to pull it back to fire the arrows, much more so than the shortbow, but the arrows can go further."

"We all took it in turns to fire the longbow, seeing who would fire the arrow the furthest. Mr Atkinson's went the furthest, but out of us, Tim won and I was second," said James.

"Nice one!" said Liz. "One good at accuracy, the other distance. A good pair." Jenny and James both pulled faces.

"It was good fun, but really makes you think how much everything has changed in just a few hundred years," said James.

It was dark by the time dinner had been eaten and a pair of pupils had been selected to wash and dry the dishes. Following instructions, they all put their coats and boots back on and went out and round to the back of the hostel.

A roaring camp fire was blazing in a stone circle, around which was a circle of tree trunks, laid down to make seats. A little bit away, in the darkness, water could be heard and Barrie, shining his torch, saw a stream running parallel to the length of the hostel that looked like it would join the gorge they'd walked along earlier.

"We can build a dam across it this week," said David, appearing next to him.

Morton was tending to the fire and they all sat round in groups, chatting and watching the flames, seeing faces and patterns in the fire. The teachers sat together and said they had until nine o'clock then it would be bedtime.

As the flames burned down and the embers glowed brightly, Mr Atkinson brought out the marshmallows and, sticking skewers through them, everyone enjoyed the hot sweet sticky treat.

"I want a photo of this," said Liz, reaching into her coat pocket and pulling out her phone, the other three leaned in for a selfie.

"Rats, my phone!" exclaimed Barrie, realising it was still in Morton's bag.

Looking round he couldn't see Morton anywhere and asked David who was monitoring the fire where he was.

"He's had to nip off I'm afraid," said David, "his nan isn't very well and so he often visits her in the evenings."

Barrie immediately thought of Nain, his own precious nan and felt a pang of sympathy for Morton.

"Can I help?" asked David.

"It's nothing," said Barrie, not wanting Miss Martin to overhear about his phone.

Returning to the others, he told them, adding he'd wanted to message his dad.

"It's OK," said James. "That app we installed on the way up will tell my phone exactly where yours is. If it is in Morton's bag in his room, we can ask David to get it."

"Oh, excellent," said Barrie, and looked at James' screen as he opened the app on his phone. A green dot showed where James' phone was currently, and the two could see the outline of the hostel clearly on the map.

"Yours will be a red dot," said James, selecting Barrie's number, and they both looked as a red dot appeared. "Well, it's not in the hut," said James, zooming the map out to understand where the dot was.

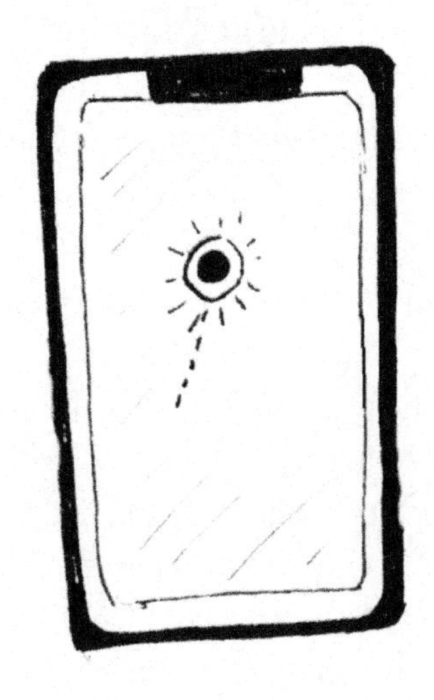

Barrie looked, tracing the line of the gorge with his finger. "Oh no!" he exclaimed, lowering his voice quickly as the teachers looked up. "It must have fallen from Morton's bag. And I was so careful to zip it right up."

"What do you mean?" asked James.

"Well, that red dot is right about where we were climbing and abseiling at Flittermouse Cliffs. It must be lying there. Oh I'm going to be in so much trouble. Are you sure it's current?"

"Hang on a minute," said James, zooming back in on the red dot. "Yes, it's current all right, but look!" he said, pointing. Barrie looked. The red dot was moving.

"Your phone hasn't fallen out," said James. "Morton's bag must be moving near Flittermouse Cliffs."

"But if he's there, what about his nan?" asked Barrie. "She's ill and he's visiting her."

"Well, unless she's a bat, he isn't," said James. "So why go to a cliff face in the complete darkness, and why lie about it?"

Jenny and Liz, who'd been listening, leaned in, little prickles of excitement running up their necks.

"Your gut feeling may be right, Bar," said Liz, and Barrie nodded.

"Flittermouse cliffs, what is your secret?"

Chapter Seven

Suspicions are Raised

That night, Barrie tossed and turned in his bunk. Why had Morton returned to the cliffs? Why had he lied, saying he was visiting his sick nan? What was going on? It was after midnight when he finally fell asleep, and even then, he dreamt of bats flying from cliffs, so when Mr Atkinson banged on the dorm door at half past seven, Barrie was still half asleep.

James, on the bunk below, hooked his feet up to press on the underside of Barrie's bunk. "Come on sleepy head," he called, joggling Barrie with his feet. Barrie grunted and dropped down from his bunk. Most of the other boys had headed to the shower block, so it was quiet enough for them to have a quick chat.

"I just have question after question popping into my head and no answers," said Barrie. "It's so frustrating."

James nodded. "I was thinking about it too," he said. "It could be of course, that Morton was going to see his nan, and that it was the route he took. We just caught a snapshot of him."

"I guess it's possible," said Barrie, doubtfully. "Though it didn't seem to be moving very fast."

"True, and I wish now I had kept watching it on my phone," said James. "By the time I thought to look again, your phone was moving back down the path."

"What time was that?" asked Barrie.

"About half past ten," said James, "I took a screenshot." He got out his phone and showed Barrie. The red dot was just the hostel side of the woodland scramble section.

"So about two hours since we saw it first," said Bar, thinking. "I guess if it was a shortcut that might give enough time, but, oh, I don't know."

Other boys returning and Mr Atkinson giving a five minute warning for breakfast effectively ended the conversation and the pair hurried to wash, dress and brush their hair.

With bowls of cereal and ice-cold milk, the two boys slid into chairs across from Jenny and Liz.

"Morton is back," said Jenny. "Our bunk looks out onto their hut; he and David were out early putting helmets and buoyancy aids into piles."

"I wonder how his nan is," pondered Liz, crushing her cornflakes with her spoon.

"If he actually went to see her," said Barrie, quietly.

"If you slip out to get your phone, you could ask him, Bar," suggested James.

"Good idea," replied Barrie, and shovelled his cornflakes into his mouth.

Jenny and Liz were facing where Miss Martin and Mr Atkinson were sitting. As Barrie finished his last mouthful, Jenny whispered, "Go now, they're deep in conversation, we'll say you've gone to the toilet if asked, and if you go to the ones at the hut while you're out too, we won't be lying."

Barrie slipped out and quietly left the hostel. He crossed to the wooden hut, there was no sign of Morton or David, so he went round to their living area. David was there, eating some toast.

"Morning, Barrie," he said. "Everything OK?"

"Yes thanks," said Barrie, his eyes scanning the hut. "Is Morton around, please? He was looking after something for me."

"He is somewhere about," said David, spreading butter on more slices.

Footsteps could be heard and Morton appeared, smiling, carrying a kettle. He plugged it in and picked up a slice of the freshly buttered toast.

"Hello Barrie, out early. Did you enjoy yesterday?"

"Yes, thank you," replied Barrie. "It was really great. I'd love to learn to climb more. I forgot to ask you for my phone when we got back yesterday. Do you have it, please?"

"Of course, sorry, I completely forgot about it," said Morton, crossing to his bag. Unzipping the top pocket, he brought it out.

"Here you go," he said, handing it to Barrie. "It's another no phones day today as we're on the water, so best go and put it in your dorm."

"Thank you," replied Barrie, putting it into his pocket. "I'll do that." He turned to leave and paused, wondering how to bring up Morton's night time activities.

"I, er, David said your nan was ill..." he said awkwardly, "I do hope she is better soon, my nain is amazing. I love her massively and guess you do yours."

There was a fraction of a second's hesitation by Morton, so brief, that had Barrie not been studying him so closely, he would have missed it.

"Ah, thank you. Yes, she is lovely but just a bit under the weather. I have a bit of supper with her, and it cheers her up. You had better go and get ready."

Barrie left Morton eating his toast, most questions in his head, heading via the shower block in case he was spotted.

Barrie found James by their bunk. "Got it, but it's flat," he said, plugging the phone in to charge.

"What did he say?" asked James, pulling a jumper over his head. Barrie told him, and about the slight pause.

"I'll ask him too, then," said James. "Dad said when they interview suspects, they often will ask the same or similar questions a few times to check if they are being truthful. It's a lot harder to keep to the same story if you're making it up, as you have to remember each time what you have made up."

"Clever," said Barrie, pulling his jumper and coat off his bunk.

James went outside and, as everyone began appearing and chatting, he seized the opportunity and wandered across to where Morton was taking some paddles from the hut.

"Can I help you, Morton?" offered James, reaching for some paddles.

"Thank you, er?"

"James."

"Thank you, James," said Morton, passing James some more paddles. "Can you pop them with the helmets and vests?"

James dropped four paddles by the kit and returned to the hut where Morton was bringing out some more.

"I was sorry to hear about your nan," said James, taking a paddle and waiting for Morton to pass him more, "I hope it's nothing serious."

"Thank you, she's a bit under the weather, so I often go and spend time with her."

James thought quickly to what Barrie had said, under the weather, supper, it was all checking out so far. How else could he test if Morton was lying?

"Is she far away from here?" asked James

"Two villages away, not bad," Morton passed him three more paddles and James took them to the pile. David had appeared and was beginning to kit people up with helmets and buoyancy vests.

The teachers had also appeared and Mr Atkinson smiled as he saw James helping. James gave an embarrassed half-smile back. There would only be one more set of paddles to get. He thought fast, searching for a question that would prove or disprove any legitimate reason for Morton being at Flittermouse Cliffs last night. Returning to the hut he thought he may have it.

"Two villages sounds far away, how do you get there?"

"I er, catch a bus," said Morton, with the smallest of hesitations, but sharp James had noted it and continued.

"Gosh, I can't imagine a bus out here. Where do you catch it from? How do you get to the bus stop?"

Instead of answering, Morton responded with a question which caught James off guard. "Why all the interest?"

James had to think quickly. "I was just wondering if Mr Atkinson could take you in the minibus while we're here. I'm sure he wouldn't mind."

"Oh," said Morton, pausing. "Very kind thought, but I'm sometimes quite late and I wouldn't want to put anyone out."

"He could perhaps drop you at the bus stop?" pressed James, imagining how his dad would interrogate Morton.

"It's OK, honestly, I er, I get it from just along the main road."

"At the end of the track?" asked James, pointing to the stone track their minibus had brought them in on the previous day.

"Yes, it isn't very far and I enjoy the walk. Here's the last lot of paddles. Get kitted up and we'll be off. I'll join you in a minute."

James did as instructed and joined the others at the front of the hostel. It was a bright sunny day and, for October, seemed quite warm. Everyone was dressed in their thick coats nonetheless, knowing how cold it would be if the sun went in.

David was helping them all get the right sized buoyancy vests and helmets, checking each one for fit. Liz and Jenny were already wearing theirs and it reminded James of how they'd looked in the summer. Barrie was just finding a helmet and James was soon also adorned in helmet, and vest.

"Pair yourselves up and everyone grab a paddle," called David, fitting the last of the vests on Mr Atkinson. "Please do not use them as pugil sticks, we don't want to be taking anyone to hospital."

David continued to outline the morning's activities ahead, checking everyone could swim and confirming that no one had their phones on them. They were to spend the morning kayaking, which pleased the four greatly. Divided into their pairs, the four stood close in a huddle, eager to know if James had found anything out. As David paused, James almost just breathed the words, "Morton's lying."

The other three all leaned in closer. "How do you know?" hissed Liz.

"Catches bus down track, main road," whispered back James, trying to keep his lips still. "Nowhere near Flittermouse Cliffs."

It wasn't until the briefing was over and they were walking about half a mile downstream to the kayaks that the four could comfortably talk

"I deliberately asked Morton where he went to visit his nan and how he got there," said James, elaborating on his earlier comment. "He said it was two villages away and that he caught a bus from the end of the track we drove in on."

"So, in the complete opposite direction to where he actually went?" asked Barrie.

"Yes. But he was a bit suspicious, asking me why all the questions. I had to really think fast and said something about Mr Atkinson giving him a lift. No idea why that popped into my head."

"Good job it did, though. Fancy using your nan to lie. That's just wrong," said Barrie, thinking of his own precious nain, and how he could never do such a thing.

"I wonder what he's up to?" asked Jenny, puzzled, to herself as much as anyone.

"No idea," said James, "but I'd love to try and find out."

The other three nodded. Yes, just what was going on?

Chapter Eight

Back in Kayaks

Arriving at a wide, calm stretch of river, the four saw a collection of two person kayaks similar to those they had used at Barrie's in the summer. Morton talked through a safety brief while David ably demonstrated actions as Morton described. They really did work well together - like a double act.

At last they were all assisted in getting into the kayaks. Just as they had in the summer, Liz and Barrie shared a kayak and James and Jenny shared another. It felt great to be back on the water, and everything they had learned during that week in Wales came flooding back.

Morton congratulated them on picking everything up so quickly. "Looks like we have some pros already! Great going, guys!"

Many of the others were still trying to not hit each other with the paddles, and yelling as they got splashed in the face with cold river water.

Mr Atkinson, sharing a kayak with Sky, replied to Morton. "They made the national news with their canoeing adventures in the summer."

David looked up. "You're not the kids from Wales? Hall with a funny name, some type of owl?"

The four smiled, self-consciously.

"They are indeed," beamed Mr Atkinson, he was very proud of how the four had developed since starting at Grey Owls last year.

"Wow. I read about you. That's amazing! What a small world. You'll have to tell us everything around the campfire tonight. I didn't know we had celebrities among us."

Awkward grins could be seen on each of the four's red faces, as they each remembered back to the summer.

"David does seem very nice," said Jenny to James, paddling away. "I hope he's not mixed up in anything."

"So do I," replied James. "Morton seems nice too, there's just something about him I can't put my finger on."

"You sound like Bar," laughed Jenny, quietly hoping for an adventure.

It didn't take long for everyone to master the basics of controlling the kayaks, and Morton declared they could head off down river and play some games.

Morton and David each had a single person kayak, Ryan was in a kayak with Miss Martin and, looking at them, Jenny thought how he was often with her. Possibly so he has to behave, pondered Jenny, who still felt angry about his behaviour before the trip.

Soon they were all paddling slowly downstream. Morton would shout commands and they all had to race to complete the task.

"Right bank," sent them all paddling to the right.

"Left bank. Stop. Back paddle. Spin!"

It was great fun, and hard work, taking up most of the morning, enjoying playing on the river, the commands getting faster and faster.

They were then split into two teams. The four again found they were on different teams. "So as to not give unfair advantage," said Morton.

David had continued downstream to where they would be stopping for lunch and each team had to pass a large foam baton between each of their four kayaks as they paddled down the river. The baton had a loop at one end, attached to which were three carabiners. Each pair had to remove a carabiner, so that in the end every kayak should have in it either a carabiner or, if the final pair, the baton. The first team to David, having passed it between all, would be the winner and would get a prize that night. Any team to David without passing the baton between all would forfeit their win. Blocking the other teams' kayaks was permitted, but not using the paddles on people.

It was chaos. The pupils, all screaming and yelling excitedly as they careered down the river, two brightly coloured foam batons being waved, and then thrown between kayaks.

David was half a mile downstream by a wooden jetty, ready to take photos on a robust camera he and Morton were documenting the activities on, and smiled at the hysterical laughter that accompanied the eight kayaks as they came into view, jostling for the lead.

The team with Jenny and James in was ahead by a fraction and, despite valiant attempts by Mr Atkinson and Sky to block them, David declared them the winner by the narrowest of margins.

They continued downstream, where, unlike the river near Tully Hall, they had to negotiate small waterfalls.

"Listen to how to get down safely or you'll end up like Matthew Waddington did last year," said Mr Atkinson.

Everyone had paid full attention, remembering the bruises and cuts Matthew had sustained to his face when his kayak rolled over.

It was thrilling, carefully steering the kayaks through the white water that tumbled over rocks and crashed over boulders. Leaning back as each kayak nosed down the waterfalls, there were wild screams and shouts from everyone, even Miss Martin.

David, positioned further down, was busy with his camera, getting impressive action shots as each pair came down, to forward onto the school.

There were three waterfalls to negotiate, each one larger than the previous. Rachel and Emily came very close to tipping over on the final one, accompanied by a crescendo of "Whoas!" as the rest watched them fight to stay upright.

The four thoroughly enjoyed it, and Barrie wondered if there were any stretches on the river by his home like this. They had only explored a relatively small section and this was great fun.

Safely through and, after some more games on the water, they all hitched up to a mooring point.

Phil and Pete were on the bank to meet them and helped get the kayaks out of the bank and onto a big trailer that was hitched behind a red minibus on some hardstanding near the river.

Everyone was ready for lunch after the morning's exertions. Large packs had been in the instructors' kayaks and, much to everyone's delight, contained lunch in the form of Mr Atkinson's 'legendary' sandwiches.

"You have a choice," he announced proudly as if about to read the specials menu in a top restaurant. "Jam, peanut butter or chocolate spread. Fillings that wouldn't spoil if they had a quick dunk."

Noises of disgust were heard at the thought of soggy sandwiches, with Morton reassuring everything they were perfectly dry.

With an hour for lunch, the four found a quiet spot on the bank and were able to talk more freely about James' update.

"I hope we're not wrong and his poor nan isn't really ill," said Barrie, "I'd feel dreadful."

"Let's look at what we know so far," said Jenny.

"Well, I saw the pathway in the cliff," said Barrie. "Unused for the whole year, but with a shiny new carabiner part way along."

"Morton kept looking at it," said Liz

"Bar's phone showed Morton at Flittermouse Cliffs after dark," said James, "and it didn't return for over two hours." This was news to the girls.

"Morton has told us he was visiting his sick nan two villages away, and that he gets there by bus," continued James. "He catches the bus from the end of the track we came down from the main road on, in a completely different direction to Flittermouse Cliffs."

"So what don't we know?" asked Jenny.

"We don't know how long he was at Flittermouse Cliffs for," started Barrie.

"We don't know what he was doing there," said Liz. "Quite possible, I guess that he likes bats and had gone to watch them."

"In the dark?" asked Jenny.

"He may have night vision goggles," said James. "You can get them."

"We don't know if he also saw his nan," said Liz, always keen to see the best in people.

"Do you think we'll end up a group that can just sniff out adventures?" asked Jenny, thinking of all the wonderful stories she could write.

"It still may all be nothing, he may just like walking in the woods at night, or having some time away from the noise we all make," said James. "But I hope not."

"Me too," said Barrie, and the girls nodded.

Mr Atkinson came to join them and asked what they were so engrossed about.

"We were just talking about Morton's nan," said Barrie, thinking quickly. "And how sad it is that she is ill."

"Ah, yes, David mentioned that," said Mr Atkinson. "I do hope the dear lady is OK."

They all made sympathetic sounds, even though they suspected the 'dear lady' was perfectly fine.

"Time for your next adventure," announced Phil, standing up from the knot of instructors and gesturing to the minibus. They all piled in, wondering what would be next.

Phil drove them first to a large stone barn where the kayaks and paddles were being stored for the winter.

"Normally we just moor them back up where you started, but it'll be about five months until they're used again so they're safest locked away and out of the weather."

The barn reminded the four of that at Pen Y Bryn, and Liz kept a sharp eye out in case there was a cat that she could fuss over. To her disappointment there was not one to be seen and ten minutes later they were back on the road, heading up into the wilds of Northumberland.

Wonderful hills and green spaces opened out as the minibus rumbled up narrow lanes. After only about ten minutes, Phil pulled into a parking area by some trees and turned off the engine.

"Right," said David. "This afternoon we're going to have a go at orienteering. Has anyone done this before?"

There was silence.

"Excellent. Who has used a compass before?" he asked. Again, there was silence, no one had, nor it turned out, had they read a map.

"OK, well, you might find your way back by Friday in time to go home," he joked.

"Everything's on our phones now," said Tim, a little defensively. "Map apps will tell me where I am."

"That is true," replied David, smiling. "But map reading is a really good skill to have, even now with phones and apps. What if the battery goes flat, or you drop it and it breaks or lands in water? If you can manage to navigate with a map and a compass, you need never be lost. Nowadays there is a thing called geocaching. It uses GPS and is a worldwide activity, so if you enjoy today and want to do more with technology, you might want to look that up." James made a mental note to look up if there was any geocaching around Grey Owls that they could do during the weekends.

"The aim today is to get from here to the finish point in the shortest time. You will be going via some locations where there are stamps or punches to mark your cards and show you have done the whole route. You need to divide yourselves into three groups of four."

Jenny, Barrie, James and Liz automatically moved closer together.

"Won't we all just follow the fastest group?" asked Sky. "That will be easy."

"Nice try, but no," laughed David.

"Each group gets a different map with a different route and checkpoints. Each route is about the same length, around five miles," explained Morton.

"So if you sort yourselves into groups of four please, we'll give each group a map, compass and card to mark, and away you can go," said David.

All the children looked horrified, not knowing how to use them. David paused, looking round at their worried faces with a mischievous twinkle in his blue eyes.

"Oh, yes. We will give each group one other thing to help you. You'll each get one of us to teach you how to use everything as we go. We'll show you how to use it to set off in the right direction, and then you'll navigate the rest of the way between you and we'll just help if needed."

As pupils arranged themselves into groups, James, Jenny, Barrie and Liz huddled closer and avoided making eye contact with the teachers, hoping they wouldn't get split up. To their relief they were left as a group and Pete joined them to be their guide. The other two groups had David and Morton, with Phil driving the minibus to the finish point. Miss Martin and Mr Atkinson joined the other two groups.

"Are we the winning team?" asked Pete, smiling and gathering the four around a map. A dotted line was drawn across it in a rather haphazard fashion. "We are here," he said, pointing to the start of the dotted line. He lined up the needle on the compass with north, explaining as he did, and turned the map so north on the map pointed with north on the compass. The four quickly realised which way they were to go. Jenny pointed northwest up the steep hillside.

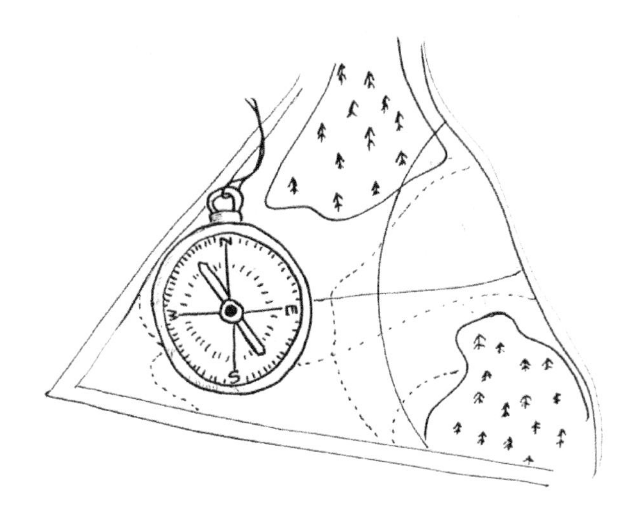

"Spot on," said Pete, folding the map. "Let's go."

They set off at a brisk walk, heading away from the other two groups who were both starting to walk south.

Up and up they walked, trying to hurry as much as they could but finding it steep and tough going. Pete kept getting the map out as they came across path junctions and handed Jenny the map as they came to an upland barn.

"First checkpoint," he announced, helping Jenny locate it on the map. The four looked around the barn and soon spotted a hole punch tied to a post by the corner of the barn wall. James retrieved the card he was carrying in his pocket and stamped the punch next to 'Checkpoint 1', it made a star-shaped hole in the card.

Jenny looked at where they were to go next, and pointed on up the hillside. "It can't possibly be much higher," panted Liz as they continued climbing. "We're going to run out of hill!" It did indeed seem that they were walking to the sky.

"Don't worry," said Pete, easily matching her stride. "We're nearly at the next point."

Reaching the top, they saw a stone pillar rising up out of the ground. They rushed to it and saw a brass plate fixed into the top of it.

"Is this it?" asked Barrie and Pete nodded. The four looked around and quickly saw the second punch, which James marked the card with.

James looked at the brass plate. "What is it?" he asked.

"It's a trig point," explained Pete. "These are found all over the country at the highest points around. They were used for mapping the country. There is another one way in the distance on that hill top there," he added, pointing over to a distant hill. The four could just make out a small lump on the horizon.

"It certainly has an amazing view," said Jenny, "I wish we'd been allowed to bring our phones. I would have liked to take some photos."

"Ah, yes. We had to get quite strict with phones when we're doing anything near water or on the rocks. They are so expensive and so many were getting damaged, it was just too much trouble. Plus, a lot of the time people were too engrossed in their phones, they weren't listening to the safety briefs and they were more likely to hurt themselves."

"We'd not damage them here though," said Jenny.

"True, but in the past people have cheated at this, using the app on their phone instead of the map. I'm sure none of you would, but there is also something about just being present here, enjoying the outdoors without being a slave to technology." The four could all relate to that. They all enjoyed being outside and in nature, though Jenny still looked a little glum.

"Here, use this," said Pete, getting his phone out of his pocket. "My phone for emergencies, but if you'd like to take some photos, we can Bluetooth them, or send them to your phone later."

"Oh, great, thank you," said Jenny, beaming as she was handed the phone and took several photos of the stunning scenery. "Can you please take one of the four of us by the trig point?" she asked, as James, Liz and Barrie all stood round it giving wide smiles and thumbs up.

Pete did so and then suggested they had a go at working where the next checkpoint was.

"It's looking like the next two are on a winding track heading towards the fifth, which looks like a castle on the map," said James. They all looked round, certain something as big as a castle from their elevated viewpoint would be easy to spot. There was nothing to be seen however, and, using the compass and map to orient themselves, they headed along the ridge before dropping down a track. Along the track was the third checkpoint, then they dropped into a wood towards checkpoint four.

Barrie kept checking the map and Liz, wearing the compass round her neck, shouted their direction. The wood was huge and dense, with trees which had been there for hundreds and hundreds of years. Tied to a magnificent old oak tree was a bright orange ribbon, at the other end of which was a punch; the fourth checkpoint.

Continuing down the track, checking the map, Jenny, in the lead called back. "We're nearing the edge of the wood, it's definitely thinning."

Emerging into the daylight the four found themselves almost on top of the castle.

"Oh, wow!" exclaimed Jenny, quite lost for words for once. It was a ruin of a castle, but nevertheless very impressive. Built of grey stone, it faced defiantly down the hill, as it had done for centuries.

"Arrow slits, look," said James, pointing to the walls. They all gazed up at them, imagining how many arrows had been fired through them from inside the castle in years gone by. There was still a large, studded oak door at the front which Pete took them to for their fifth checkpoint, and James stamped their card.

"Can I please take some more photos?" asked Jenny, Liz nodded, she'd like photos too.

"Sure, but we won't win if we stay long."

"We don't mind, do we?" said Barrie, who would rather enjoy exploring than race around not really seeing anything. The others agreed and explored around the castle as Jenny took some photos of them and the ruins.

Liz had a go at map reading,

"Looks like down there?" she asked, pointing down a track that led over a stile and across a grassy field.

"Yes, well done," said Pete and, as Jenny handed his phone back, they all headed off, jogging downhill to make up some time.

They took a wrong turn to the last checkpoint and ended up on the wrong side of a stream. Pete stopped them trying to wade through and, retracing their steps, they found the little stone bridge and the last checkpoint. From there, it was not far to the finish point.

Rounding a corner of a barn, the four were pleased to see the red minibus waiting for them, with the other two teams gathered around it.

"I think my legs will drop off," said Jenny, "That's been excellent fun though," and the others agreed, they had enjoyed learning a new skill, and felt tired and content.

"All aboard for your ride home," called Phil, and they all piled in, exhausted.

Sitting together, Barrie reflecting on their lunchtime conversation, thought about all they'd discovered and how many questions they still had to answer.

"You know, in twenty-four hours, we've found out quite a lot," he ventured. "But can we answer any of the unknowns in the next twenty-four hours?"

Chapter Nine

The Boys are in Trouble

Arriving back at the hostel, James and Barrie helped Morton and David put away the helmets and vests as Pete and Jenny transferred the photos onto her phone before he and Phil disappeared off in the minibus.

Barrie had suggested to James on the way back not to mention Morton's nan, in case it brought suspicion, they would just try to get to know him better and see if he let anything slip.

It didn't take long to stow the kit and the conversation stayed around the day's activities and a request from David to hear all about their summer adventure around the campfire that evening. Neither James or Barrie could detect anything odd about Morton.

The two joined the other pupils getting cleaned up and ready for dinner where Mr Atkinson, who had declared himself cook for the week, proudly served up a pasta bake and salad.

The four sat together as usual and discussed what, if anything, they could do.

"Morton seemed normal, friendly and chilled," said James,

"If he wasn't, people would notice though," said Barrie. "And we're only seeing really subtle things."

"Or imagining them," said James. Barrie, convinced there was something going on, rolled his eyes.

"I think," he said, chewing on something in the pasta bake he couldn't quite identify, "I think we should keep an eye on Morton, and if he slips off, we should follow him."

"It'll be a bit obvious," said Jenny. "Four of us tramping along behind him. He'll hear us or see us."

"And we'll be missed here," said Liz.

"We won't all go then," said Barrie, developing the idea in his mind. "Two could stay here, covering for us."

James, sat deep in thought, was warming to the idea. "That could work," he said, in a low conspiratorial tone. "From now on, all of us watch Morton like hawks."

The others started feeling excited again, even if this turned out to be nothing, it was thrilling to be spying.

"Who will go?" asked Jenny. "We can see their hut from our bunks and be look out."

"That is excellent," said James. "Bar, how about you and I follow, and the girls 'keep obs'?" Barrie nodded, and Liz felt ever so important, 'Keep obs' sounded so formal and serious.

James and Barrie volunteered to do the washing up and drying; it gave them quiet time to plan what they'd do.

"We'll always have an eye on him. If he heads off, we need a good excuse to slip away if we're in company," said Barrie. "I'll ask you to help me with my phone. You're so known for that, so it won't cause suspicion."

"Good idea," said James, passing Barrie a clean, wet bowl for him to dry. "We'll take torches, but try not to use them," he added, thankful they had brought the ones they'd bought in the summer with them.

"And our phones," said Barrie. "We may need to call the police!"

"Or the girls," said James. "Better remind Liz to charge hers, it's always nearly flat."

"Yes, we all need to be able to message each other if he goes." The group chat the four had set up would be ideal for this, Barrie thought.

"I think we're pretty much planned," said James, letting out the water. "Now all we need is for Morton to go off."

Miss Martin appeared at the door, thanking them for washing up and sending them outside with a chocolate each.

Behind the hostel, the campfire was already lit. It was not quite dark and the flames danced up towards the sky, twigs crackling in the heat. David was over by the stream, while the boys could see Morton showing a small group how to tie different knots.

"It's really important to get the right knot," he explained. "Especially when climbing. The wrong knot could end up with a nasty fall. That's why you should never climb like we did, and will tomorrow, unless you're with someone who knows what they're doing."

James and Barrie spotted Jenny and Liz, standing with the group by the stream listening to David, and sat on a log by the fire to wait for them.

Jenny and Liz passed smooth, flat rocks to David who, wearing wellies, stood in the middle of the small stream. He placed the rocks carefully in a line under the water across the stream from one side to the other. More and more rocks were handed to him from a pile that was on the bank.

"If we create a bit of a dam here, it will make a bit of a deeper pool and should capture some of the creatures that live in the stream. We can check the pool tomorrow night and Thursday and see what's swimming there."

"What sort of things will we see?" asked Liz.

"Nothing is guaranteed," said David. "We may not see anything, but hopefully there will be some beetles, perhaps some small fish and if we're really, really, lucky, we might see a white-clawed crayfish."

"A fish with claws?" asked Sky.

"It's not really a fish," explained David. "It's like a miniature lobster. They are only a few inches long, and quite rare now."

"Why are they rare?" asked Liz.

"A larger American signal crayfish species was introduced back in the 1970s, it nearly wiped them out."

"I'd love to see one," said Liz.

"Fingers crossed, then," replied David, and both Liz and Jenny immediately crossed theirs.

Once the rocks were above the water height, making almost a narrow walkway from one bank to the other, David climbed out. Saying they would check the following night, he walked off towards a pile of chopped wood.

The girls joined James and Barrie on a log by the roaring campfire. Barrie discreetly checked their phones were with them and charged - they were.

David, setting down an armful of firewood sat near them and Morton, his rope knot demonstration finished, sat next to David.

"So, tell us about your fabulous summer adventure," said Morton. "David says you're quite the heroes."

They began, starting with how they went to stay with Barrie and his family in North Wales, and how they learned about priceless silver going missing, and decided to try and solve the mystery of its disappearance.

They all took turns at telling parts, and both David and Morton asked questions and seemed really interested.

They had just got to telling about the barn discovery when Morton's phone beeped and they paused, in silence, as he read a message.

"I'm really sorry, I've got to nip off," he said. "And it was getting so exciting. Will you tell me the rest tomorrow please? I'd love to hear it."

"Everything OK?" asked David, looking at Morton.

"Yes, just Nan wanting me," replied Morton, standing up.

"Would you like me to drive you somewhere?" offered Mr Atkinson.

"No, thank you," said Morton, a fraction too quickly. "Very kind, but I'd not deprive you of enjoying such a tale."

"Poor Morton," said David, watching him go. "He often has to go and see his nan, makes for long days. But carry on with your story guys, I'm hooked."

They did, though a little more rushed as James and Barrie now needed to get on Morton's trail.

Jenny and Liz took on most of the talking at the end and, as they started on what happened after, with the police and television, James and Barrie made their excuses and slipped back to the dorm.

"It's been ten minutes, long enough for him to be a safe bit ahead of us if he went to Flittermouse Cliffs, even if he didn't go straight away," said James, pocketing his torch. "Let's go."

They slipped out, watching keenly in case either of the teachers had returned inside. Disappearing into the darkness, the boys moved silently, straining their eyes and ears for any sign of their quarry.

Unbeknown to them, however, they had been spotted, and by someone determined to spoil their plans.

Ryan had seen the two slip away and saw a perfect opportunity to cause trouble for the pair. He grinned in the darkness, revelling in the chance to get his own back on Barrie after he'd exposed Ryan as the note writer.

As James and Barrie walked quickly up the track along the side of the gorge, Ryan debated how long to leave it before telling his tale. He didn't know why they'd gone, or how long they would be gone for, only that they were out of bounds; the hostel and area behind it being where everyone had to remain. If he left it too long, they may be back and that lovely opportunity would be wasted. He must tell now, he decided.

Ryan quickly went to Miss Martin and asked if he could speak with her. Getting up from the campfire, Miss Martin moved a few feet away from the light of the fire to listen. Just at that moment Jenny, on her way back from the shower block and unseen by either Ryan or Miss Martin, overheard Ryan telling tales on the boys, and appearing to take great delight in doing so. She stood horrified. What a beast Ryan was!

Quickly and quietly passing by them, she grabbed Liz up from by the fire.

"Need you a min," she said, pulling her along. "Ryan saw the boys go. He's just told Miss Martin. We have to do something."

"I'll message them and get them back," said Liz, already getting her phone out and unlocking it.

In under 20 seconds, she'd written and sent a message.

GET BACK NOW. Miss Martin knows you've gone.

It was an anxious time as they waited for confirmation the message had been read, and then a reply.

On way

Liz sent a further message quickly.

Say you went looking for owls, we'll try cover, putting her phone away as Miss Martin approached them.

"Have either of you seen James or Barrie?" Miss Martin asked, studying them closely. "They are not in their dorm."

"I was in the shower block, they were by there," said Jenny, thinking it was not a total lie, they were technically, just a bit further away. "Perhaps they're in the shower block, or near there, listening to owls," added Jenny.

"We must search for them," said Miss Martin. "I cannot have children going off. Out of bounds means out of bounds for a reason. Anyone found breaking the rules is in big, big trouble."

Jenny and Liz looked at each other as Miss Martin stalked off to Mr Atkinson. The poor boys, what could they do?

Liz sent another message

Hurry

Jenny caught sight of Ryan out of the corner of her eye, he was wearing a smug expression. How horrid he was.

Miss Martin and Mr Atkinson quickly checked the hostel and shower block, Miss Martin fretting at possibly losing two children on her first residential trip. They were just about to leave David in charge and head off searching when James and Barrie appeared, out of breath and panting.

Miss Martin was fuming.

"Where have you two been?" she demanded, furiously. "You know not to go out of bounds."

The two boys, looking extremely contrite, apologised, saying they'd caught sight of a creature in the night and wanted to identify it. Technically Morton was a creature, they reasoned. Out of sight, Jen gave her tawny owl impression. It really was very realistic and reminded Barrie of the girls' suggestion.

"It was probably just an owl," he said. "I am sorry Miss; we didn't intend to cause alarm and weren't far away."

James added his apologies, both boys stopping short of promising not to go out of bounds again.

"Go to your dorm for the rest of the evening," said Miss Martin, still very angry. "If you're caught out of bounds again, you're going home. Have I made myself clear?"

Sitting on James' bunk in the dorm, the boys used the group chat to update the girls on what had happened and learned of Ryan's attempt to cause trouble.

James and Barrie thanked the girls for the warning and said they'd seen a torchlight some distance ahead at times, and were sure Morton was again heading for the cliffs.

The trouble now was, not only did it appear they may indeed have a secret to unravel, but they had an enemy within, who would be trying to catch them out. They had only one chance to find out the secret, or they'd be sent back to Grey Owls in disgrace.

Chapter Ten

Flittermouse Cliffs - Part Two

Wednesday breakfast was quite tense for the four. Ryan kept sneaking looks over to them and Mr Atkinson, serving James and Barrie toast, had said how disappointed he was that they, of all pupils, had broken the rules and gone out of bounds. They both apologised again and James, who hated others to find fault with him, found he could barely eat any breakfast; he felt quite anxious and stressed.

The other three, in their usual way, when any one of them was down, rallied and reassured him.

"It could be important," said Liz. "Sometimes, it's about doing the right thing, not doing things right," she added, sounding much older than her twelve years.

"We just will have to be more careful," said Barrie. "Now we know Ryan will watch for us, we can take account of that."

"I'd be so very ashamed to be sent home," said James, imagining how mortified his mother would be, and disappointed his father. They had been so supportive of him getting the scholarship and so overjoyed at his behaviour and courage in the summer, he just couldn't let them down. Liz seemed to read his mind.

"It's OK, James, if we need to follow Morton again, you can stay and be look out and I'll go instead. Then you don't have to worry about being sent home."

James smiled his appreciation, thinking how lucky he was to have the three.

"Let's take each day as it comes," said Barrie, keen to change the subject and take James' mind off last night.

"Dad says the cow byre roof is nearly finished. He's sent me pictures, look." Barrie produced his phone and they all looked, a feeling of familiar contentment washing over them; they'd helped clear that byre.

"Gosh, it looks so different," said Jenny. "What's made it look so... I can't put my finger on it."

"Windows," said Liz, pointing to the white window frames that now graced what had previously been open holes in the stone walls. "And the gutters have been painted."

"The roof looks smart," added James, seeing the, once sagging roof was now straight, re-slated and watertight.

Barrie beamed with pride. "Dad's pretty much done it all," he said. "With a local man helping with the slate roof tiles. He said he wanted to get it watertight and weatherproof by the winter so that he can concentrate on the inside through winter and start letting it as holiday cottages in the spring. Next in is the plumber, I think. Dad said something about ground source heating, he's trying to keep it as eco-friendly as possible. You will have to come and see it when it is done." The other three all nodded enthusiastically, they would love to be back at Pen Y Bryn farmhouse.

After breakfast they were split back into their two groups from Monday. The group that Liz and Barrie were in headed off with Pete and Phil, who had appeared at the hostel that morning, and Miss Martin to have a go at archery.

James and Jenny, with their group, went over to a pile of helmets and harnesses, where David and Morton helped them pick the right sized kit and checked it once on. This morning, it was their turn to climb and abseil down Flittermouse Cliffs.

Barrie had explained carefully to James exactly where he had seen the carabiner, and had even sketched the position of it from ground level. James and Jenny would both be keeping their eyes peeled.

Liz and Barrie arrived with the others at the archery ground. Pete and Phil took them through the history of archery, at it being a method of hunting first.

"We're so slow compared to most animals, we'd never stand a chance really trying to chase something and catch it. Prehistoric man would have made tools instead. This is what separates us from most other animals. He would have made spears to throw and bows and arrows."

"Can you still hunt with bow and arrows now?" asked Miss Martin.

Peter shook his head. "No, not in the UK. Bowhunting was banned in, I think 1965, so no playing Robin Hood, though in other parts of the world they are still used. By some tribes it is their primary means of getting food."

"Is there such a thing as a poison arrow?" asked Barrie, who was sure he'd seen something about them on a programme.

"That's a really good question," said Phil, impressed by the level of interest being shown. "Yes, there was and poison arrows are still used today in several areas."

"So where do they get the poison from?" asked Barrie,

"It varies between areas. I do know that the indigenous South Americans use the poison dart frog. They rub the frog's skin which secretes the poison onto their arrow tips and blowpipe darts."

Ryan pulled a face of disgust, not wanting to rub a frog against anything, least of all a poisonous one.

"It's how they hunt and survive," said Phil, seeing his expression. "Not everyone has shops to visit like we do."

Phil then went on to tell them about the use of bow and arrows in mediaeval England, as battle weapons rather than just hunting.

"Those arrow slits we saw yesterday in that castle must have made you pretty safe to stand behind and fire through," said Liz.

"Yes, exactly," nodded Pete.

"Let's have a go then," said Phil, picking up a shortbow and demonstrating how to hold and fire it.

The targets were set as they had been on Monday, at forty, seventy and one hundred yards. It was a lot more difficult than it looked, though Phil and Pete both made it look almost effortless. The children were very much in awe.

Barrie managed to hit the blue ring on the target at forty yards and, after several attempts, the red ring at seventy. Liz couldn't get closer to the centre than the black ring, but she was just proud to have hit the target.

There were arrows whizzing through the air, arching up before falling to earth.

"Don't they make an amazing sound?" said Liz to Barrie as he took aim and fired,

"Yes, it's a weird whistle isn't it. And it's a nice 'thunk' when they hit the target," he replied.

Miss Martin, it turned out, was somewhat of a natural and beamed at the applause as she hit the gold centre of the target.

Barrie, keen to redeem himself with her, clapped louder than anyone and gave a "Whoop". Miss Martin looked at him and smiled, and he felt his anxiety drop a notch.

Miss Martin also was reflecting on the evening's events. Had she been too harsh on the boys, who had only been missing for about ten minutes in the end? She felt such a responsibility for them, but also wanted to be liked herself and had been so impressed by their bravery and teamwork in the summer. But then, she was still in training. She couldn't afford to have a bad report from the school, and them arriving back out of breath meant they had to have been tipped off, so who knows how long they'd have been gone for had the alarm not been raised by Ryan. They had to not go out of bounds again. So, while she would make an effort to be friendly towards them, the threat of being sent home would stand and would be carried out.

Ryan, keen to maintain Barrie's anxiety, took every chance to pull faces at him when Miss Martin was not looking, and mouth the words, "Going home."

The longbow was next and James had been right about it being a lot harder to pull back than the shortbow. Liz struggled and Pete put his hand over hers and helped her draw the arrow back and fire it. Neither Barrie or Liz could get anywhere near the furthest shots and decided, if they ever needed to go into mediaeval combat, the shortbow would be the weapon for them.

Liz had been right when she'd said Jenny would love the gorge with all the autumnal trees.

"Oh, wow. Just look at the silver birch," marvelled Jenny, her mouth open in wonder. "Their white trunks against the oranges of their leaves are so stark. It's almost like their skeleton. Magnificent. Morton, do you have the camera? Could I borrow it please?"

Morton had heard from Pete on the journey back from orienteering about Jenny's passion for pictures and, smiling, passed her the camera.

"It's nice isn't it," he said. "I often like to walk up here if we have a quiet time."

"Quite magical. It's calm and peaceful with the trees and all the different colours of their leaves, yet dramatic with the rocks and rushing water in the gorge. I love it."

They all continued up, through the dense woodland section before returning to the gorge side.

The sound of the water tumbling over the rocks on the bed of the gorge was oddly soothing.

"Almost hypnotic," thought James. He would sometimes listen on an app to the sound of flowing water if he couldn't sleep at night.

"Gather round," David's voice cut through James' day dream and he moved to where everyone was watching as David fastened a rope to his harness and explained how the climb would work.

Jenny looked with interest at the numerous horizontal fissures and crevices in the rock face, imagining them all crammed full with bats. She shuddered, focusing back to the climb.

Morton, the belay fastened to the front of his harness, released the rope out as David climbed, keeping it fairly taut once David had fastened a quickdraw between the rope and an eye bolt.

Even though she was expecting it, having been told by Liz, Jenny still jumped when David let go of the cliff and dropped a short distance, suspended by the rope with Morton preventing him from dropping any further.

David, the safety fall demonstration over, continued his climb to the top, leaving a trail of chalk handprints behind him.

"OK," said Morton. "Who will be top belayed first? You have to take out the quickdraws as you go."

James, wishing he could climb as well as David, who had obviously been climbing for years, volunteered. Although his skills of science and technology kept him inside often, he loved any opportunity to get out in the country, away from cities and modern life and he felt excited as the rope was fastened to his harness.

He was quite tall for his age, and so could reach the same hand holds that David had used, carefully unclipping the quickdraws and fastening them safely to the back of his harness. The climb felt very comfortable and James was surprised to find himself at the top quite so quickly, he wished the climb had lasted longer.

"Well done!" said David, warmly, "That was a really nice climb, you're a natural."

James was pleased. David let the rope down and Mr Atkinson climbed next. He'd climbed on each trip but preferred to keep his feet firmly on the ground, so it was quite a stilted, slow climb.

Jenny, deciding to climb last, took the opportunity to ask Morton about the bats in the cliffs. After all, they didn't know why he seemed to frequent the cliffs at night, he may have a genuine interest in the bats that live there.

Morton, however, seemed to know very little about the bats. "Brown ones," he replied when Jenny asked him about what types they were, and didn't know anything about when they hibernate or what they ate. Jenny had done a bit of research on her phone the previous evening to be able to test any answers he gave. She surprised herself by being pleased at his complete disinterest in bats, perhaps she wanted an adventure more than she'd realised.

When it was just Jenny and Morton left at the bottom of the cliff, Jenny realised, almost as if for the first time, that she'd have to climb. Although she'd seen the others all climb up, some slower than others, but all making it to the top, it seemed an impossibly steep rock face now.

"I don't think I can," she said to Morton, feeling worried.

"You can," he bobbed down beside her. "Never let the fear of failing at something stop you from having a go."

Jenny managed a tentative half smile. "What if I get half way and can't get any further?"

"That won't happen, but you would just be lowered very carefully back to the ground. We'll look after you. It's normal to have a bit of nerves. Have a go?"

Jenny nodded and, checking the rope was attached securely she went to the foot of the cliff.

"Climbing!" shouted Morton up to David, who took the slack from the rope.

To her surprise and relief, it was easier than she had thought it would be, and with only a few pauses as she searched for suitable hand holds, Jenny made it safely to the top.

James congratulated Jenny as she rolled over the top onto the path, thumping her on the back and giving her a hand to her feet. She wore a triumphant expression and felt so pleased to have managed it. Morton climbed up next, and they set off on the short walk to the abseil point. Jenny discreetly updated James about Morton's bat knowledge, or rather lack of it, James raised his eyebrow. Bat watching as a possible reason looked out, then.

Reaching the abseil point, as he'd done for the group on Monday, Morton carefully demonstrated how they could safely control their descent and slowly edged backwards over the side. Jenny felt a bit funny in her stomach seeing that, and hung back, to watch the rest go first.

Mr Atkinson was the first to descend after Morton. He tried to hide his fear by singing loudly on the way down, causing laughter from the top as he got the words and tune all mixed up.

James went next, eager to see the carabiner that had caused so much intrigue.

He went steadily down and, as he came level with the path of bolts going up and to the left on his left, he stopped, pretending to adjust his chinstrap. He scanned his eyes discreetly to the left and saw the silver birch tree and the bolts leading to the crevice, exactly as Barrie had described. There was one thing different, though. The carabiner was gone.

Chapter Eleven

Liz Makes a Shocking Discovery

Over a lunch of sandwiches and fruit back at the hostel, Jenny and James told Barrie and Liz about the carabiner's disappearance. Jenny had also looked out for it on her way down and had not been able to see it.

Barrie was immediately full of questions. "What was Morton like? Did you ask him about the bolts?"

"We didn't ask him," said James. "He knows now that we four talk all the time, it would have raised suspicion."

"I did ask him about the bats," put in Jenny. "He's completely clueless, and it seemed quite genuine."

"What was he like when you were abseiling down?" pressed Barrie.

"I came down first after Mr Atkinson," said James. "Jen had climbed last to give her a chance to ask about the bats. Morton was photographing everyone as they came down and chatting with Mr Atkinson. He did perhaps give the odd furtive glance towards the bolted path, around the silver birch, but whether that was just me wanting to see something..." he tailed off as Miss Martin called them to all hurry up, put coats and boots on and head out to the minibus. An afternoon on the beach was planned, with a fish and chip supper. Liz was very much looking forward to having her favourite treat. She loved haddock and chips, with lots of tomato sauce.

They headed off to the dorms to get ready and Barrie packed a parcel of Nain's flapjack into his pocket for the four to enjoy that afternoon.

Soon they were all in the minibus, joined by David and Morton who insisted on singing songs which they all joined in, even Miss Martin, and they got louder and louder. By the time they got to the beach they were all very giddy indeed.

"Wow. What a beach." Jenny gazed around in wonder, a huge wide expanse of white sand, stretching as far as the eye could see. In the distance she could see a castle, facing the sea in almost defiance, she would love to visit it someday.

Mr Atkinson, seeing her looking at it smiled. "We'll be visiting there on Friday morning on the way home," he said and Jenny smiled back, she loved castles.

It was certainly different to the small, rocky coves she had known all her life in Cornwall. The sea seemed miles away and Mr Atkinson informed them it was still now going out.

"Tide doesn't turn until four o'clock," he said. "So, we can have plenty of time for fun and games, sandcastles and sketching. I've bought some pens, pencils and pads if anyone would like to do a spot of drawing, but first I thought we'd all enjoy a game of rounders." Flourishing a round bat and ball, he strode off and they all followed across the beach to a sheltered spot by some dunes, where everyone dropped their bags.

Four bags were arranged in a large square to make the four bases of the rounders pitch. It was played a lot at Grey Owls and was an energetic game of two teams. One team would field while the other team took it in turns to bat, much like in cricket. Instead of running up and down a pitch between wickets, the batter, having hit the ball, had to run as fast as possible round all four bases and back to home. If they got round in one go, they scored a rounder, worth ten points. If they hit the ball or indeed missed it, and it was caught before it hit the ground, they were out of the game, and if they missed the ball but weren't caught out, they could only go to first base. The fielders, while the batter was running, had to get the ball and then had two choices. If they threw the ball to the bowler, the batter had to stop at the next base they were running to. However, if they got it to the base the batter was running to before they reached it, either by throwing it to another fielder or running with it, the batter was run out and out of the game. As soon as the bowler threw the ball, always underarm, to the next person in bat, everyone on the batting team out on the pitch at bases could then run on, scoring a half rounder worth five points if they made it home without being run out.

The teams would swap over either when every batter was out, or after a fixed time. Grey Owls normally had each batter bat a set number of times or the game could go on for hours.

David and Morton headed up each team which would play, selecting their players. Liz and Jenny were together on one team. After some cajoling and encouragement, both Miss Martin and Mr Atkinson took off their coats and joined a team each. Jenny and Liz were on the team which won the coin toss to bat first, with David and Miss Martin. Jenny, after scoring a half rounder on her first bat, missed the ball that was bowled to her on her second and was caught out by Mr Atkinson, stood behind the batters, fielding as backstop.

Liz had better luck. As she stepped forward to bat, numerous cries rose up from the fielding team; "Leftie!" The fielders all scrambled to reposition themselves on the other side of the pitch. Liz was left-handed and so would hit the ball, on the rare occasion that she didn't miss it, to the right instead of to the left like most right-handers.

The ball connected with her round bat with a resounding thwack and, without waiting to see where the ball had gone, Liz threw the bat down and raced off round the bases, her long blonde hair waving wildly behind her like a flag in a strong breeze.

Her lungs and legs felt on fire, but her teammates were cheering her on and, over the rush in her ears, she could hear Jenny screaming, "Run! Ruuuuun!"

Liz was approaching third base fast. She had to gamble on trying for a rounder and risking being run out, or playing it safe for a half. Trusting her teammates, she summoned up every bit of power in her legs and, as the fielding team threw the ball back to the pitch, her arms and legs pumping, Liz threw herself past the fourth base and home. She tumbled onto the sand, breathing hard as her teammates cheered. Running on sand was much more difficult than running on grass, everyone was finding. By the end of their batting turn, everyone having batted twice, David's team was on 100 points, a tough score to beat.

Then Morton's team went in to bat. David was elected to bowl and took it very seriously, with good humoured rivalry between him and Morton. He sent the ball down the pitch with real spin. Two of Morton's team were caught out by the backstop and not many were managing to hit the ball. After the batting team had all batted once, and were trailing 30 points to 100, Miss Martin asked David if she could have a go at bowling.

To the relief and delight of Morton's team, Miss Martin was no bowler. She jogged a couple steps, then stopped, and gave the most gentle of underarm throws anyone there had ever seen, giving the batter plenty of time to see it coming and respond.

The gap between the scores began closing, with a lucky catch by Tim taking Mr Atkinson out.

As Barrie stepped forward for his last bat, and the last bat in the game, they were only twenty points behind David's team. Sky and Ryan were both at bases and so, to draw, they'd both have to get home this ball and Barrie would have to score a rounder. Anything less and David's team would win.

Miss Martin rubbed the ball in her hands, building up the tension. She focused on Barrie's bat and threw a gentle underarm ball towards him. Barrie watched it come, bringing his bat forward to meet it. The ball struck the round bat at an angle and shot off in an unexpected direction. Jenny and Tim both set off after it in hot pursuit as Barrie ran for first base and Sky and Ryan also ran for home. The ball had bounced and was rolling. Tim was nearly with it but someone else had seen it. Someone who was faster than Tim. A small, scruffy haired black dog had spotted the ball and, just as Tim was reaching down for it, dashed in front of him and grabbed the ball in its mouth, racing off joyfully with it towards its mortified owner.

Everyone, batters and fielders alike erupted into helpless laughter at the proud little mongrel sabotaging the last ball of the game. Barrie, knowing he now had all the time in the world, did a comical little dance between the third and fourth base as the owner tried desperately to wrestle the ball from the dog's mouth. He crossed fourth base and home to a hero's welcome, saving Morton's team from defeat.

As the ball was thrown back by the embarrassed owner, while she struggled to restrain her dog, David caught it deftly and announced the game a draw. No one had any energy left in their legs to run anymore and heartily agreed that it was a worthy draw.

Finding a quiet spot by another dune and flopping down on the sand, pulling their coats up around them against the fresh sea breeze, Barrie produced the flapjack and the four munched contentedly.

"Your nain really is the greatest," said Liz, nibbling her piece like a little rabbit to try and make it last longer.

"She loves it!" said Barrie. "She really missed you all after our week there, we'll have to see if we can all go back to mine again."

"Yes," said James. "That would be great, though I'm very glad we've come here for this week. Well done, Liz, for coming along."

Liz grinned, a little embarrassed. "I wouldn't let you down," she said, grateful for all their support. "It's great fun." she didn't share that she still felt homesick at night and had counted down, just two nights left. "I need to get a postcard and send it to Mum and Dad," she added. "There's a little shop I saw on the main street by the beach entrance. I saw it on the way in."

"I don't know why you don't do what I'm doing," said Jenny, tapping her phone, "I'm sending Mum and Dad an e-postcard, completely free. That photo I took of us all at the trig point looks great as a card. The one I took of you by the castle yesterday would be a great one to send."

"Mum still has the one I sent her from Wales on the fridge. I'd like to send her a real card," replied Liz. "I did send her some of the photos you took yesterday, but it's not the same as a real card."

"You can order real ones on your phone," suggested James. "If you don't want the walk. My legs are all done in after all that running. I'd happily help you with the app."

"Thanks James, but I'll go and get one. There may be one with that castle on."

Liz got up and, leaving the other three resting on the sand, she went to where Mr Atkinson, Miss Martin and David were sitting and asked if she could go to the shop and get a postcard. David confirmed that it did sell postcards and stamps, and added that there was a post box just outside it.

Ryan, sitting close by, muttered that postcards were for old people to send. He'd intended just for Liz to hear, but the breeze caught his words. Mr Atkinson looked at him sternly and declared postcard writing to be a lovely activity to do. He said Liz could go and even lent her a pen to write with.

Liz took the pen and set off across the beach and up to the main street. It was quaint and the small village shop she'd spotted had a little bell that rang when the door opened. Liz went inside and smiled at the row of glossy, local postcards, some showing the beautiful castle. She picked one, the castle with a stunning sunset behind it, and paused, seeing a tea towel with sketches of local places on it. Barrie's nain would love that, she was sure, and it would be so lovely to get her something as they'd agreed; a thank you for all the baking she had done and sent.

Liz opened her purse and took out the money her mum had given her as pocket money for the week. She counted up what everything would cost and smiled, she should just have enough, though the card may have to go second class; she wasn't sure of stamp prices.

The shop keeper, a small, grey haired gentleman, served Liz and told her there were picnic benches down the side of the shop used for people to enjoy ice cream at in the summer.

"You can sit and write your card there," he said. "The last post goes in about half an hour, so you have timed it well."

Delighted with the tea towel, full of pleasure at the thought of showing it to the others, Liz thanked the man, left the shop and went down the side to a wooden trestle table and bench.

She began to write to her mum, consciously not putting anything about Morton, just that the gorge and Flittermouse Cliffs were beautiful, and that she wished her mum was there to enjoy it. As she paused, thinking of anything else to say, Liz heard a man's voice, clearly angry, but trying not to shout.

"What the hell did you supply me with?" almost spat the voice.

Liz stopped thinking of what to write and pricked up her ears.

"Yes," came the voice again, they must be talking into a phone, she thought, only one side of the conversation could be heard. "I sold some to Stevo, Monday. Yes, it's serious, it's in the paper!"

There was a pause. "It is. I'm reading it on the billboard thing." The voice was very agitated, but there was something familiar about it

Liz, all the hairs on her neck standing up with excitement, quietly got to her feet and, holding her breath, crept as silently as she could down the side of the shop. She could hear someone pacing up and down the pavement. Ducking back and crouching down behind the post box, Liz tried to make herself as small as possible in the hope she wouldn't be noticed.

What was all this about?

Daring to risk peeking out, she recognised who she thought the voice had belonged to. Morton was striding up and down, a phone pressed tightly to his right ear. He hadn't spotted her.

Liz suddenly thought of her phone. If it rang, or a message came through, it would give her away. She wished she'd put it on silent. Getting it out now would surely alert Morton to her.

"It was never meant to hurt people. Just make some extra money. I'm not up for people getting hurt. Especially kids," said Morton in hushed tones.

There was a long pause as whoever was on the other end replied. Liz realised she was holding her breath. She thought she would burst.

"The big shipment on Thursday. It had better be decent and clean." There were a few more mutterings Liz couldn't quite make out, possibly the word midnight, then Morton ended the call.

Miraculously, Morton didn't look Liz's way, but rammed his phone and hands into his coat pocket and strode off towards the beach.

Liz waited till she was sure he'd gone. What had made him so angry? What had been sold and what was this about a shipment? She stood up and crossed to the little 'A' frame board with local news headlines. Liz hadn't noticed it before, being so focused on the postcard. The side facing her was blank, but what she read on the other side made her draw breath in shock.

TWO TEENS IN HOSPITAL.
POLICE WARN OF DANGEROUS TABLETS

Liz couldn't believe what she was reading. Drugs? She must tell the others about this. It sounded like Morton was indeed a 'bad lot' as her mum would say, but what was more, lives were in danger.

Chapter Twelve

A Conference

Liz's mind was working in overdrive. She had to get back to the others! Drugs! This was huge! So, had Barrie been right from the start perhaps? There was something about Morton.

Liz was about to race off back to the other three when she remembered the postcard, still sitting half written on the table.

'Now at the beach, see you soon, Love Liz x' she scribbled, shoving it into the post box with excessive force.

Fighting the urge to run, Liz walked as fast as she could back to the beach. She was conscious that, if she arrived back from the shop out of breath, it would perhaps attract questions, perhaps alert Morton that he'd been overheard.

She was about to message the others and tell them she had news, but as she drew her phone from her pocket another thought struck her. What if they read it when Morton was present and reacted? It wasn't worth the risk, she had to be patient.

By the time she rounded the sand dunes to where the other three were sitting, Liz was ready to burst. She was just drawing breath ready to blurt it all out when the sight of Miss Martin sitting with them stopped her in her tracks.

Miss Martin had chosen that moment to speak more with Barrie and James about their disappearance. While she had every confidence in their ability to be safe, given their record, it was the risk of others copying and going off that was the problem. It was for that reason that the rule of being sent home if they went out of bounds again must stand, no matter how wild and wonderful the reason. She didn't care if it was the biggest mystery on earth. Not while she was in charge.

Liz quietly got out her phone and sent a message to their group chat.

Think I know what Morton's up to.

Jenny felt her phone vibrate and was the first of the three to check. Her eyes widened, which Barrie and James both saw, and understood must be something exciting. They emphatically agreed with Miss Martin, apologising again and saying they completely understood her position, desperate to get her to leave them so they could find out what had made Jenny so amazed.

Miss Martin seemed keen, however, to stay and chat. It was only when Mr Atkinson, who'd been sat sketching the castle with a small group, appeared, announcing it was time to begin the walk to the chip shop which was expecting them, that she finally got up off the sand and began rounding up the others.

Barrie and James, both looking at their phones, turned to Liz with questioning expressions.

"Morton was by the shop," hissed Liz.

"Come along everyone, a brisk walk for a fish and chip supper," boomed Mr Atkinson, appearing by them.

Barrie scowled at the sudden intrusion. He, more than anyone, wanted to know if his hunch about Morton had been correct.

Liz didn't dare say anything else. There were too many ears close by. It would be dreadful if someone overheard and the secret was out before they had a chance to discuss it.

Shepherded on the walk along the seafront to the fish and chip shop, the four were in constant close company and, to their disappointment, the arrangement of tables where they were eating meant they could not sit alone and chat safely.

The food was fabulous, and the large white flakes of haddock, plump golden chips, sprinkled with salt and vinegar, did in some way make up for them being unable to discuss Liz's news. Liz had squirted ketchup over her chips and was concentrating hard on them, enjoying every mouthful, while replaying the overheard conversation again and again in her mind. Everyone was tucking in heartily, David and Morton cracking jokes and generally being the life and soul, friends to all.

Liz did manage to discreetly send another message:

Wait till properly alone. Too big not to tell all.

On reading it, James, Jenny and Barrie felt almost unable to contain their curiosity. This sounded extremely important. Liz was not the sort of person who would exaggerate.

Anyone could have been mistaken for thinking they were looking at a line of penguins travelling along the sand in the fading light as the pupils and adults waddled back across the beach to the minibus. Everyone's tummies were full and they felt tired and content, all aside from the four who were full, tired and impatient to be alone.

During the minibus ride back to the hostel, Liz produced the tea towel she had bought for Barrie's nain and they all loved it, with Barrie saying his Nain would definitely treasure it. David, seeing the gift, explained where some of the places printed on it were.

"It was a lovely shop," said Liz. "I'm just ready now for a laze by the fire."

"I don't think we're having a fire tonight. I believe Mr Atkinson has something else planned," said David.

Mr Atkinson, hearing his name mentioned, looked in the rear-view mirror and smiled. "I've got a surprise in store!"

The four smiled back politely. They weren't really interested in a surprise, unless it was to do with the mystery. All they wanted to do was get together in private and hear Liz's news.

Arriving back at the hostel just before dusk, the four were about to try and slip away when David called. "Let's check the little dam. Who's coming? Liz?"

Liz had been so keen the day before, now she felt conflicted. On one hand she was excited to see if there was a crayfish in the pool, on the other she was desperate to tell the others what she'd overheard. Faltering, she felt Jenny give her a little push.

"Come on, it'll look odd if you don't," she said, and they both went round the back of the hostel to the little stream with a few others.

"Everyone else, you've got half an hour to rest and relax, send any updates to your parents or guardians, then be out at the front in walking boots, warm clothing and coats."

"It'll be dark!" protested Sky, who felt more at home surrounded by bright city lights, than the pitch black of rural life.

"That's the idea, Sky," replied Mr Atkinson. "If you have torches and want to bring them, do, but you won't need to."

James and Barrie, not quite as animal obsessed as Liz, headed inside to lie on their bunks. The fish and chips were sitting heavily and they both felt quite lethargic.

David, putting wellies on and with a small hooped dipping net, stood in the middle of the stream, by the makeshift dam. The small group of children gathered round, all eager to catch a glimpse of the rare crayfish. David dipped the net carefully into the pool the dam had created. Sweeping it slowly across he drew it out, everyone leaned forward. The net was empty.

"Let's try again," said David, undiscouraged, and put the net further down into the pool. Bringing it up, everyone could see something wriggling inside the net. Was it the rare crayfish?

David pushed up the bottom of the net and there, supported by his hand, was a small silver fish with a brown back. It was only about the length of half a pencil.

"What is it?" asked Liz, leaning forward to take a closer look.

"A fish, dopey," teased Jenny, "and I thought you were into animals."

The group all laughed and Liz gave her friend a good-natured shove. "I know that, I meant, what type."

"It's a three-spined stickleback," said David. "Look at its back, can you see the three spines?"

Looking, Liz could clearly see the spines sticking up in front of its delicate fin.

"Yes. Is it rare?" she asked.

"No, one of our most common freshwater fish, I think, but still lovely to see," replied David. "Let's let him go."

David submerged the net downstream from the dam and the stickleback swam out, completely unharmed.

"Wish I'd taken a photo," said Liz as the little fish disappeared from view. "Is there anything else?"

David looked again and swept the net about, but there was nothing.

"We'll look again tomorrow," he said, climbing out. "You'd better get ready for Mr Atkinson's surprise."

Liz and Jenny returned to their dorm for ten minutes before they were due to assemble at the front. There was too much coming and going so they both sent their parents messages, telling them briefly about the day and the dog running off with the ball.

"Gather round everyone!" called Mr Atkinson, flashing his torch about from the front of the building. All the children moved in closer.

"We're going on a short night walk up to an open space to do some star gazing." he announced excitedly.

"Thought your mum had said they weren't doing night walks anymore," whispered Jenny to Liz.

"She had. Mr Atkinson must be doing his own thing."

"Northumberland is fabulous for stargazing. There are not the same levels of light pollution experienced in many other parts of the country. It's a bit of a passion of mine."

The stars seemed to fit together with maths and physics, so the revelation of it being an interest of Mr Atkinson's came as no surprise to the four.

"We're going to walk away from the gorge, past the archery field and just up the next hill so you can enjoy an uninterrupted view and learn some of the constellations."

"The what, sir?" asked Sky, not sure this was really for her.

"The constellations," repeated Mr Atkinson. "The names for some of the groups of stars. Let's go!"

With that he strode off in the direction of the bridge over the gorge and they all followed. David and Morton had torches, but the moon was so bright it was easy to see enough without them.

On the walk over, Liz was able to finally share with the others her discovery by the village shop.

"He was talking into his phone in a really agitated way," she explained. "Stomping up and down, up and down. I heard him say "What the hell did you supply me?" she continued, her voice rising slightly with excitement.

"Shh," said James, concerned that, despite the group being spread out, someone may overhear her, although he was keeping a sharp eye-out.

Liz continued in a whisper. "He was saying how it was serious, and that it was in the paper."

"What was?" asked Jenny.

"I'm getting to that bit," said Liz, enjoying finally being able to tell the tale. "Morton didn't say, but he said the next shipment on Thursday had better be clean, it is a big one or something."

"Shipment? What of?" asked James, almost to himself.

"When he had gone, I looked at the board with the news headlines on. Two teenagers were seriously ill after taking some tablets."

All three gasped. This was very serious indeed!

"So Morton is into drugs!" said Barrie, his eyes wide in disbelief. "I knew there was something odd about him, wouldn't have guessed drugs, though!"

"This is really important. You have done brilliantly, Liz. Can you remember anything else he said?" asked James.

Liz paused, thinking hard. "I'm not sure as it was muffled and he was walking away from me, but when he was talking about Thursday, I thought he said midnight, but I'm not one hundred percent."

James suddenly coughed loudly; he'd seen Miss Martin approaching.

"Are you four into stars?" she asked, a gust of wind blowing her dark hair across her face.

"No, not really, but I'm sure it'll be fun learning." replied James, and the others mumbled similarly, frustrated at the interruption. Annoyingly, Miss Martin stayed with them for the rest of the walk.

Arriving in the field, Mr Atkinson looked up at the night sky. It was clear and there really did seem to be more stars than usual shining out against the inky black sky.

"There. There is the plough," said Mr Atkinson, gesturing them round him and pointing as he described a rough square of four stars with three leading off from it.

"Looks more like a saucepan to me," suggested Tim.

"It's actually sometimes called that, or the Big Dipper, or the Great Bear, which is what the Latin name for what it is part of, Ursa Major, means. I've just always known it as the plough." They all stared up.

"Now, follow up from the front of the saucepan, as you put it, straight up from those two stars. You see the next bright one?" he pointed, showing the line they were to follow, "That is the pole star, or north star. Polaris is its proper name. If you are facing that, you are facing north."

They all dutifully followed his gaze and found it.

"Continue that line," explained Mr Atkinson, raising his voice against the wind which was beginning to gust more. "And you'll see something that looks like a smaller upside-down plough. That is part of Ursa Minor, the Little Bear or Little Dipper."

A few large drops of rain began to fall, which seemed odd as the sky was clear. Turning, no stars were visible to the south and west as great rain clouds began to blow in.

"I think perhaps we may have to cut tonight's star gazing short," suggested Morton to Mr Atkinson, seeing the children turning to face away from the wind. "This wind was not forecast till later tonight, but it seems no one told it."

His face looking crestfallen, Mr Atkinson nodded and announced to the group: "Back we go then. Nobody rush, and we'll all have a mug of hot chocolate as a treat in the lounge."

The wind was rising and prevented any discussion other than brief shouted comments on the way back to the hostel. The clouds had made it a lot darker, making everyone grateful for the torch lights. The four hadn't brought theirs, wanting to save them in case they needed them for tracking, so stayed close to the others to avoid tripping up.

Back at the hostel, with damp hair, everyone took off their wet coats and boots, before piling into the lounge. Mr Atkinson, keen that his young stargazers should have enjoyed the evening, quickly boiled up some kettles of water. Adding generous amounts of drinking chocolate to jugs, he poured everyone steaming mugs of hot chocolate.

David and Morton bid them all goodnight, heading out into the wind to secure anything that may blow away in the night.

Miss Martin yawned loudly and that set the others off. It had been a long day, jam packed with activities, and everyone was feeling tired.

"Bed time I think," she announced and, even though it was early, no one complained.

The four all needed to talk more about Liz's discovery so, under the covers as the wind continued to howl in the night, they continued to discuss Liz's discovery by message.

Should we phone the police, asked Barrie. There was a pause as the others typed their replies.

We could. But would they believe us? replied Jenny.

An instructor that looks at a cliff face a bit funny, a forgotten carabiner that could have belonged to anyone, and a nan who may or may not be real... It doesn't sound much, typed James.

Not when you put it like that replied Barrie, with the girls liking his comment.

I honestly don't think we have enough evidence to go to the police at the moment, typed James.

Tell a teacher? asked Liz.

I think after her chat with us today, Miss Martin would think it was a tale we had invented to try and get allowed out. I got the feeling she wouldn't believe anything we said. Plus, we run the risk of spooking Morton and it all being for nothing, replied James. Barrie replied that he'd got the same impression of Miss Martin following the chat.

I vote we see what we can find out tomorrow, suggested Jenny.

I think we will have to try and discover the secret ourselves, typed Barrie.

Tomorrow at midnight will be our only chance, replied James.

Shivers of excitement ran up all the three reading that. They would have one chance to discover the secret of Flittermouse Cliffs - tomorrow at midnight. The question now was, how?

Chapter Thirteen

Plans are Made

It seemed to Jenny that her eyes had barely been closed for five minutes before Miss Martin was knocking on the dorm door and calling them all to dress in one layer of clothing and get in for breakfast. The group chat had continued sporadically until almost midnight as thoughts kept entering restless minds, and Liz was asked to repeat in the chat everything she could remember hearing.

Liz felt as tired as Jenny and yawned loudly as they got dressed, padding sleepily into breakfast.

It was obvious James and Barrie had not slept well either. Both had hair stuck up, James had an odd tuft at the front and Barrie's curls looked more unruly than ever.

Some of the tables used for breakfast had already been pushed to the side and in the space they left, Morton and David had laid out a large selection of wetsuits and were helping those who had finished breakfast find a suit that fitted.

"Don't forget, you are to wear your old shoes that you were told to bring," said Mr Atkinson. "They won't get spoiled but will get wet. Oh, and take your towels over to the shower block and leave them there."

It was far too busy and crowded to be able to discuss the discovery of the previous day, so the four concentrated on getting their suits and shoes on, and heading outside to join the others. David and Morton were out, helping everyone find helmets and life vests that fitted. The wind had, thankfully, died down completely and the day was bright and sunny.

"We'll be heading off soon, and the plan is to walk up to just past where we did the rock climbing and abseiling and enter the gorge there. Then we will come back down, mainly scrambling, sliding and wading down the gorge itself," explained Morton.

"Where I come from," added David, "it's called ghyll scrambling, so you may have heard of that, but round here, it's known as gorge walking."

There was excited chatter as pupils exclaimed at getting into the cold water.

"Won't we freeze?" asked Rachel.

"Not at all," said Morton, smiling. "The neoprene wet suits you have on will keep you warm and we will all be moving most of the time. We will travel down the gorge, almost to here, and then hot showers and a late lunch will await you."

"My special sandwiches!" announced Mr Atkinson, to which everyone groaned loudly, and then laughed.

"If everyone's ready, we'll head off," said David. "Remember, no watches and no phones. They would definitely not benefit from today. Our camera is waterproof, so we'll capture all the action."

On the walk up, the party strung out and the four were able to have short, rather snatched conversations.

"How sure are you about it being midnight tonight, Liz?" asked Barrie, wondering how he'd stay awake after such little sleep.

Liz considered. "I'm sure he said it's tonight. Positive on that. I felt quite sure at the time about the midnight bit, but it was difficult to hear and," she paused, thinking hard. "Oh, I don't know, now."

"What are you thinking, Bar? Head out to Flittermouse Cliffs about midnight and see if anything happens?" asked Jenny.

"It's possible," said Barrie. "But if what Liz heard wasn't midnight and the shipment is at, say 10pm, we'd miss it."

Liz felt even less confident of the time, hearing that. If they relied on her and she was wrong, it could ruin everything, and they only had one chance. There was a lot of pressure on her. "I'm not really sure," she said.

James smiled at her. "Don't worry, you have done amazingly, finding out all you have without getting caught."

"Can we just maybe take turns at watching?" suggested Jenny. "Liz and my bunk face the hut, and we could leave the curtains open a bit."

"What if you fall asleep, though?" asked Barrie. "Or if Rachel, Sky or Emily tell you to shut the curtains?"

Jenny frowned, she'd not considered that.

I'm worried if we're seen keeping watch that we'll be stopped and go home in disgrace," added James.

"If Morton is taking a delivery of a large shipment of drugs or something tonight, as it sounds he is, we need to be able to catch him in the act. The question is how?"

The four fell silent as they clambered through the wooded section. A couple of trees had blown down in the night, and it was quite a scramble over them.

"Have to manage these in the dark tonight perhaps," said Jenny to Liz, taking hold of Liz's outstretched hand to keep her balance.

Barrie started to walk faster once they'd passed the fallen trees. They were nearing Flittermouse Cliffs and he wanted to see if there were any glances up from Morton.

He could just see Morton as the path approached the abseil point, deep in conversation with Miss Martin. Would he look up to the bolted path? Barrie struggled to see, being quite far back in the line. What had Liz heard Morton say, that he sold some on Monday to Stevo? Could he have climbed up the cliffs to meet Stevo at the top on Monday night? Was this a meeting point? He ducked back and whispered these thoughts to James who nodded slowly.

"It could be. It's nice and secluded. But Morton didn't say Monday night, did he? He said Monday. Could be that the deal with Stevo happened in the morning, before we arrived."

Barrie frowned, James was right.

They were bunched up in a group at the head of the gorge. It was more rocks than water, with almost natural stone steps in the side where everyone climbed down.

"Ok," said Morton, leading. "Everyone ready? You'll have to work as a team for the first part. The aim is to get to David." They hadn't noticed David wasn't with them and, looking where Morton was pointing, could see David a good way back down the gorge, waving. "Without anyone falling in. You'll have to help each other where the gaps between the rocks are quite wide. Mr Atkinson, perhaps you would like to lead off?"

Mr Atkinson did, his arms out to help him balance. They naturally began to form a human caterpillar, holding onto each other for balance as, although there were plenty of rocks to step on, few were flat enough and many were wet and slippery from being continually splashed by the water tumbling down.

Liz kept tight hold of Jenny, in front of her, who was being pulled over by Rachel, who in turn was being pulled off balance by Sky, screaming that she was going to fall in.

Miss Martin, trying to help, called: "It's like a chain of chaos. Hang on, I'm coming!" and hurriedly stepped forward onto a rock to get to Sky and Rachel quickly.

Unfortunately for Miss Martin, the foot she'd stepped forward with slipped on the steeply sloping rock and slid off the side of it, plunging into the ice water over her ankle. Miss Martin screamed with the shock and automatically grabbed the nearest person to her in an effort to save herself. Fortunately for the children, this was Morton who suddenly found himself being manhandled as Miss Martin desperately tried to keep the rest of herself dry. The scene of the two adults pitching back and forth as they tried to regain their balance was so comical that everyone found themselves helpless with laughter. Rachel and Sky, laughing so much, both slid off their rocks and into the water, yelling loudly as they did, which only made the chaotic scene even more amusing.

Liz had luckily kept such a tight grip on Jenny that she wasn't pulled in by Rachel and remained dry.

Miss Martin regained her balance, apologising profusely to Morton and helped Sky and Rachel back onto the rocks. They all continued forward to David who was laughing so hard, tears were running down his cheeks.

The rocks just beyond David were much less frequent and it was impossible to stay completely out of the water. They all picked the best path down, trying to stay as dry as possible, as the water did feel icy, despite what Morton had said about neoprene.

They passed Flittermouse Cliffs which, viewed from deep in the bed of the gorge, looked even more impregnable.

"Did we really climb that?" Jenny said, almost to herself.

Morton, overhearing, replied. "Yes, there are photos to prove it. We will give Mr Atkinson the memory card with them all on from this week and you can all have them to send to your friends and family. You've all done really well this week. Best group this year, I reckon."

There were a few shrieks from ahead as more lost their balance and ended up getting soaked. Continuing carefully down, Liz looked up again, it looked unfamiliar. There were no cliffs, but trees and great boulders came right to the bank of the gorge, only a few feet above the water. One great ash tree, right at the edge of the water, had been blown over and had hauled its roots out of the ground for all to see. She realised it was the section where the path took them away from the gorge side, and could see now why it did.

Jenny, stood near her, marvelled again at the colours and contrasts between the soft greens and oranges of the leaves and the stark grey, harsh lines of the rocks.

"I bet it looked even more dramatic in winter," she said, and Liz agreed.

"Yes, and more water from winter rain would make this gorge into a raging torrent."

"Come on you two!" called a voice and, looking up, they saw everyone stood together a short distance ahead.

"Ok. Hands up if you've managed to stay pretty dry?" asked David. Seven hands went up, including James, Jenny and Liz. "Well done, but I'm afraid you've wasted your time," he laughed, beckoning them forwards.

James, stood near the front of the group stared as the rocky bed of the gorge just disappeared, the water gushing over the steep edge in a waterfall, crashing into a pool below with a fountain of spray. He felt alarmed.

"We're all going off there!" said David, pointing over the edge, his eyes wide. There were gasps and exclamations of terror. "You trust us?" continued David, laughing more at their horrified expressions. The group all nodded tentatively. "Beneath the surface at this side, the water, over thousands and thousands of years, has carved out your very own water slide."

Looking where David pointed, they could see the water didn't shoot straight down there, in a freefall like at the other side, but flowed quickly down a steep slope for some of the drop.

"You sit here, hands across your chest, hold your breath and go," said David. "Watch."

David lowered himself until he was sat on the bottom of the gorge bed and, using a convenient rock to his side, pushed himself forward. He shot down at a terrific speed and flew off the end, landing in the large pool at the bottom, where he disappeared completely beneath the water before bobbing back up, giving a large wave. There was nervous, excited chatter at once; some eager to try, others trying still to build up their nerve.

"Just wait till David swims over and sits on that rock to take photos of you," said Morton. "Who'll go first?"

Mr Atkinson felt he had better lead by example and gingerly sat down into the icy water. "Away we go!" he shouted, and whooshed down, off the edge and into the deep pool.

One by one, they all sat down onto nature's water slide and flew down into the deep pool below. All of the four were keen to try it and eagerly awaited their turn. Morton was helping the more nervous first, so they wouldn't get wound up waiting. It was exhilarating. All the four loved it, the cold water they plunged into really taking their breath away. Swimming to the side, they congregated in a shivering mass, watching those after shooting down the slide.

David continued taking photos as each person slid down, until Morton came down after everyone and they all gathered round again.

"We've quite a scramble down to the next falls, so we'll get moving and you'll soon warm up," said Morton, and everyone headed off, keen to get moving and warm again.

The minds of the four, as they traversed down the rocky terrain, were all on how they could keep watch on Morton that night without getting seen or otherwise caught. Liz felt so sleepy, despite the thrill of the gorge walking, she didn't think she would manage to stay awake till midnight watching in the dark, and it wasn't until they were all gathered together at the top of another rocky plateau after at least twenty minutes scrambling, that a thought entered Jenny's mind.

It surprised her as it seemed so obvious. Why not plant a phone in Morton's bag or coat pocket? Frustratingly, she couldn't share it with the others as they were all gathered together looking over a sheer drop. It looked terrifying.

Without any warning, David dramatically stepped off into nothing and plunged into the pool below. In no time at all, they were all throwing themselves off the ledge into the pool, with some clambering up the rocky ledges at the side to have another go. Rachel was pleased to realise she wasn't cold at all.

With rosy cheeks and feeling proud of their courage, everyone scrambled further down the gorge, before David led them up the rocky side, and they found themselves back on the path up from the hostel.

"We'll walk back briskly to keep warm," said Morton as they gathered round and everyone followed, chatting excitedly about sliding and jumping into the pools. That had been brilliant, and they hoped David, who'd been snapping away, had managed to get some good photos so they could show their families later.

Jenny found the opportunity to talk to the other three quietly on the way back, and put forward her suggestion.

"That is a very good idea," said James. Liz and Barrie nodded.

"It's not without risks though," said Barrie. "One, we have to successfully plant it, and two he has to actually take it with him without finding it."

"Good point," said Jenny. "Coat?"

"I think he would notice it in his pocket. Maybe his bag, and hope he takes it. He took it before and might put the drugs in it to carry them back here," said Barrie.

"I don't mind putting my phone in his bag," volunteered Jenny.

James considered. "I think, if Bar is happy, it should be his phone."

Jenny looked at him questioningly.

"We know his has a signal at Flittermouse Cliffs. We don't know about yours."

"Ah, good point," said Jenny, impressed by James' thinking.

So, following Morton may be possible after all.

Chapter Fourteen

Time for Preparations

As soon as they arrived back at the hostel and began removing wetsuits and lining up for the showers, James and Barrie slipped into the dorm.

"Pass me your phone," said James, reaching under his bottom bunk for the charging cable that was plugged into the wall. "It would be a disaster if it goes flat tonight and we can't track Morton."

"Good thinking," replied Barrie, looking at his phone as he handed it to James. "It's a quarter full."

James plugged it in and they went back to join the others before they were missed. Hopefully the phone would be fully charged by the time they needed to plant it.

Showered, dried and in warm clothes, everyone piled in the lounge area for lunch, where Mr Atkinson proudly produced more questionable sandwiches with even more questionable fillings. There was a definite buzz in the air as everyone relived the excitement of the morning, overcoming their fears, shooting down stone water slides and jumping off rocky ledges into deep pools. All the other activities had been fantastic, but somehow, nothing quite measured up to the thrill of the gorge walking. It had been an excellent activity to end on. David and Morton were both there at lunch and declared Mr Atkinson's sandwiches to be the best they'd had all year, while holding up crossed fingers. David showed some previews of the action shots he'd taken, just on the viewing screen on the back of his camera

"They're brilliant!" exclaimed Sky, who'd surprised herself by how much she'd enjoyed it. "Will we get to keep them? Miss Martin, you're pulling a really funny face on the water slide."

"Yes, I'll give the SD card to Mr Atkinson when you go."

"Remember all," cautioned Morton, seeing how much they had all loved jumping into the pools. "The pools you jumped into; we know really well. We know how deep they are and that they're safe, with nothing hidden under the water to hurt you. Don't go jumping into any water you see without someone that's already checked it is safe. You could really hurt yourself, or worse."

There was a communal nod and mutter of acknowledgement. No one in the group felt they would be that daft.

"Shall we go and check the dam?" suggested David, clapping his hands together.

Liz, Jenny and a few of the others slid out from their seats and headed round to the stream, waiting while David got his wellies and net.

"I wonder what's in the pool today," he announced, rounding the corner of the hostel with his net and smiling. Liz had tried looking in, but the reflection of the moving water made it too difficult to see anything.

"A crayfish, a white clawed one. I would really love it. I'd really like to see one."

"Well, let's see what we can do. No promises!" said David, stepping into the stream. He dipped the net in, sweeping it from side to side, before drawing it out. There were some small larvae which he released downstream from the dam.

"Unlikely to have a stickleback again then, it would have eaten those," he said, dipping his net once again into the pool.

Swirling it round, he drew it out and everyone leaned in to see what he'd caught. It was empty. Liz felt disappointed.

"We'll have a last go," and in went the net again. David this time, pushed the net as far down as he could, until it was scraping along the bottom of the stream bed among the pebbles and gravel.

He brought the net up, it definitely had something in it this time, and David cupped the bottom of the net in one hand to support it as he exposed the contents with his other.

"Oh, it's all little pebbles," said Jenny, "I got quite excited."

The net had a good many small stones in it, a shining mass of browns and greys. As they looked, and David gently moved the stones, a greenish-brown shape appeared that was well camouflaged in the rocks. David quickly and gently grasped it between his finger and thumb.

"Well, what do you know!" he cried in delight. "Wishes can come true."

Putting the net down, he transferred the grasped creature into the palm of his hand. There, neatly fitting into his palm was what looked like an olive-brown miniature lobster.

Liz exclaimed in wonder: "Oh that's amazing! Is it a crayfish? A native one that is? Its claws don't look very white." Her questions tumbling out in her excitement, like the water tumbling over the rocks.

"It is indeed," said David, beaming at her enthusiasm. "Only the undersides are white or rose coloured, they are dark on the top for camouflage."

The others looked with interest, but not the passion that Liz had for all animals.

"May I please hold it?" she asked and cupped both her hands together as David carefully transferred it to her. "It's so tiny! Gosh how cute! Jen, can you get a photo of me holding it?"

Jenny quickly got her phone out from her pocket and took several shots of a very proud Liz holding the little animal, her grin wider than that of the Cheshire cat. The crayfish sat quietly, its huge claws poised in front of it, like a boxer's gloves. Jenny thought Liz was very brave to hold it so fearlessly. Those pinchers looked like they could give a nasty nip.

David took the little creature gently from her, showing her its pale underside, and lowered it into the stream onto the bed, where it quickly moved out of sight, hidden among the rocks.

"Made my day, that has," said David. "It's not often we see them."

"Made my week!" added Liz, really meaning it.

"Shall we get this dam dismantled then?" he asked, and lifted a stone from the top.

They formed a human chain and passed the rocks from one to another, the last person putting them neatly in a pile where they'd taken them from only a few days before. Liz was still smiling, what a treat it had been, seeing the crayfish. She couldn't wait to show her mum the photos.

Thanking David repeatedly, she and Jenny went inside to tell James and Barrie about the excitement. They were sitting in the lounge and looked with interest at the photos, enjoying seeing Liz so happy.

Mr Atkinson came in and announced that he was going to the nearest town to get supplies for the barbeque and that Morton and Miss Martin would be taking everyone for a walk through the woods, going down the little valley. David would begin preparing the area for the barbeque and campfire.

Two pupils, including Ryan, were allowed to go with Mr Atkinson to get the provisions and Emily and Rachel had asked if they would stay and help David, so it was a small group of eight that set off with Miss Martin and Morton.

The broadleaf woodland was a riot of colour, with greens and oranges providing a vibrant canopy. The occasional copper beech tree added its deep red leaves to the palette and holly trees provided dense green prickly columns among the bare trunks. The four, who all enjoyed the outdoors, found it beautiful and were pleased to see that, unlike upstream near Flittermouse Cliffs, the trees here had all survived the winds of the other night unscathed.

"It's a lot less rocky here," noticed Liz. "I bet their roots can push a lot deeper down and hold on better." She hadn't liked seeing the poor trees lying flat and had thought she would ask her mum and dad if they could plant a tree in their garden. She would enjoy watching it grow.

Miss Martin and Morton were happily chatting at the front, leading the way. It was a very relaxed wander and, as such, it was easy for the four to hang back just enough to stay part of the group each time Miss Martin turned her head to check, but far enough to be able to talk quietly without fear of being overheard. They needed to plan for that night.

"So, if Morton does go tonight, who is going to follow him?" asked Barrie. The response was immediate and unanimous.

"We all are," chorused the others.

"You two have already had a hard time, we are far better sticking together. We are a team. Together till the end!" said Jenny, dramatically.

James looked relieved. Being in trouble had bothered him and he was grateful for the support of the others.

"Besides," added Liz, "we might have to tackle Morton and get the police, or tackle the people delivering the shipment. We need all of us."

That made everyone go quiet for a few moments as they realised the enormity and potential dangers of what they were planning. Driven by a desire to discover a secret that may be putting other people in danger, they hadn't until now, really considered the risk to themselves.

"I still think that when you look at what we actually know, there isn't enough for the police to take us seriously. Can you imagine if they thought it was a hoax and came to the hostel? Morton would be spooked and we'd be under close watch, unable to do anything!"

"I think you're right, James. I feel like I kicked this whole thing off and, to an outsider, it may just sound nonsense." said Barrie

"Right. So, if Morton goes off, we all follow. We'll need to plan this so we don't get caught. It isn't going to be easy," said James.

"It'll be cold tonight," said Jenny. "We will need our boots and coats on. Our coats are all quite rustly. I'm worried putting them on and moving would wake people."

"We could hide them outside and put them on when we've left the hostel," suggested Liz.

James nodded. "Can you two perhaps look for somewhere we can hide them?"

Liz and Jen both nodded, pleased to be doing something active to prepare.

"Boots," added Barrie. "When we come in after the barbeque, we need to leave them at the end of the row or something."

All the boots were stored in the porch of the hostel to prevent mud from being trampled inside.

"Yes, so we can easily find them," agreed Jenny.

"I think that just leaves the phone," said James, stepping over a fallen branch. "What are your thoughts, Bar?"

"I think I'll have to try and hide it in his bag at the first chance I get. It should be fully charged by the time we're back. If I hide it in the top pocket, where I put it on Monday, hopefully he won't find it, as he obviously didn't go in that pocket when I forgot to get it before."

"That's a good idea. You could tuck it under anything left in that pocket too, in case he does go into it," said Jenny. "I know you said about Bar's phone having reception, James, but do you think I should hide mine in Morton's coat pocket in case he doesn't take his bag?"

"Hmm," James considered. "No, I don't think so, for two reasons. Firstly, he's more likely to find it, see, he had one hand in his pocket now." Looking ahead, they all saw he was right. "It would be difficult to explain away if found. If Bar's is found, I'll say we were playing a prank on him. Secondly, how would we manage to hide it? I think Morton is likely to keep his coat on all day and evening now. The chances of getting caught are just too high, and he'll get suspicious. We can't do anything that would risk that and will just have to hope that he takes his bag."

"Good point," conceded Jenny. "I'd not thought of that."

"As soon as the barbeque starts tonight, I'll take the first chance I get with my phone. And as soon as we're back from this walk, you all had better charge your phones or make sure they're full."

"Yes, good thinking," said James. "So, we have a plan, let's catch up with the others, or have we missed anything?"

"I think that's everything," said Barrie, and Jenny and Liz nodded.

"We'll have to just see what happens and do what we can tonight," said James.

Gosh, this was exciting. The four hurried to catch up, their minds racing.

Morton and Miss Martin took the group round in a huge loop and, as they emerged from the woods onto a stone track, Mr Atkinson bounced past them in the minibus, returning from shopping, pipping his horn and waving.

In not many minutes they were back at the hostel, where they were allowed some rest time before the barbeque and campfire.

"Remember, no going out of bounds," said Miss Martin to them all, while looking pointedly at James and Barrie. James immediately went red.

Jenny and Liz went off together round the hostel, looking for places they could easily and safely hide their coats. It needed to be close, but out of view of the hostel they decided, just in case anyone was awake and happened to look out as they were putting them on.

Jenny in the end found a dense holly tree. It was very prickly, but the horizontal branches made for a good natural shelf and there was plenty of space above it for the four coats. What's more, the dense foliage would keep the coats dry if it rained. It was very close, too, just out of the line of sight from the window at the boys' side of the hostel.

Pleased with themselves, they returned and told the boys who were just putting their coats on to head round the back with everyone for a group photo and the start of the barbeque.

To Jenny's delight, Phil and Pete had come to join the fun and they all crowded together as Mr Atkinson's phone, balanced precariously on a post, took a photo of them all using the timer function. It had to be attempted three times as the first two had Mr Atkinson's back in the foreground as he rushed to re-join the group.

David and Morton had already lit charcoal, and grills over the top were soon covered in food as sausages, burgers, corn on the cob and plates of mushrooms and tomatoes which sizzled as they cooked.

Morton had the tongs in his hand and seemed deep in conversation with Pete, when Barrie saw his chance.

"I'm going. Cover for me," he whispered to the others, making his move to slip away.

"Psst. Make sure it's on silent, not vibrate, silent," said Liz. Barrie nodded his thanks and, as he went out of sight he checked his phone, it was on vibrate. He put it on silent and hurried over to the hut. Now to find Morton's bag and hide it. He hoped he'd recognise it. It was red in places, he knew, but was David's also?

No sooner had Barrie gone out of sight, than the light bulb which illuminated the barbeque area went out. There were a few exclamations of surprise and shock as eyes adjusted to the dusk.

"Don't worry," said Morton. "It has a bad habit of blowing bulbs does this light. I have spares in our hut. We'll soon have light again."

This was terrible. If Morton went to his hut now, he'd bump into Barrie, and then what would happen? If Barrie was putting the phone in his bag, he'd be caught red handed.

"I'll get it for you," volunteered James, seeing the panicked expressions in the girls' faces.

Morton smiled. "That's very kind of you, James, but I know where they are kept. I'll only be a few minutes." With that, Morton handed his tongs to Pete and began to walk to his hut. Surely now he'd discover Barrie.

In complete desperation, James tore after Morton. He must somehow warn Barrie.

"Morton!" he called, "wait up!"

Morton paused.

"I wanted to ask you," said James. "How do you get into being an instructor like this?"

They walked on. "Only, I've really enjoyed this week and I think it would be a nice job, out in the fresh air," continued James, his voice getting louder and louder as they neared the hut. Cutting off any opportunity for Morton to reply, James, almost shouting, carried on: "It's been absolutely brilliant! And to do it all the time. Oh, it would be fabulous!" Surely Barrie would hear him.

They rounded the corner to the hut and Morton pushed open the door.

James, his heart in his mouth followed close behind. Was Barrie about to be caught and all their plans ruined?

Chapter Fifteen

The Trap is Sprung

Frozen in fear, Barrie had heard James' loud voice from outside. He couldn't hear what was being said, but knew it must be a warning. Someone must be coming imminently. Looking around frantically, Barrie couldn't see anywhere to conceal himself. The little hut was quite bare and functional. He heard footsteps on the wooden deck outside, seconds away, and dived under one of the beds, banging his elbow painfully. His face screwed up with the pain, Barrie wriggled himself under the bed just as he heard the door open. Hardly daring to breathe, he heard Morton and James enter.

"Well, you've clearly got your heart set on it," he heard Morton say. "Get your GCSEs behind you and then you can decide. It is a great job, physical, outdoors, and you get to meet lovely people, but it is a bit seasonal. After this week, this place shuts until March, so I have to do other work, or travel to a country that is still in season to keep doing this."

"I'd not thought of that, thank you. I'll concentrate on school then," said James, scanning the hut. Where was Barrie?

He spotted Barrie's toe end of his boot just sticking out from under the bed. What if Morton spotted it?

"This week has sort of let me dip my toe in," James continued, raising his voice on the last two words. Barrie's foot quickly and silently slid out of sight; he'd taken the hint. Morton, rummaging in a box, hadn't seen him.

"Here we go," said Morton, producing a bulb. "That's the one we need, last one too. Come on, let's get this party started."

James and Morton left the hut and Barrie let out a, rather shaky, sigh of relief. That had been too close, and thank goodness Morton hadn't noticed the top pocket of his rucksack was unzipped. Barrie had just been about to slip his phone into it when he'd heard James. Barrie wriggled out, rubbing his sore elbow. He checked again that his phone was on silent and tucked it below some walking booklets in the top pocket of Morton's rucksack. Even if Morton peeped in the top pocket, it was quite out of view.

Zipping it up fully, he crossed to the door and paused, listening for any voices outside. Fighting the urge to get out of the hut as quickly as possible, Barrie forced himself to wait until he could be sure Morton and James were out of sight of the hut. He didn't want Morton turning back and seeing him leaving the hut after such a narrow escape.

Counting up to fifty and then back down again, Barrie considered that enough time for Morton to be well away. It had sounded like they needed something for the barbeque. Cautiously, Barrie opened the door a crack and peered out. All was clear, there was no movement in the dusk, and he slipped out, closing the door as quietly as possible.

Rounding the back corner of the hostel towards the barbeque and campfire, Barrie was greeted by a cheer as the outdoor light came back on. So that was what Morton had come to the hut for.

He spotted James with Liz and Jenny who had their backs to him. James, spotting him, raised a questioning eyebrow. Barrie replied with a slow and deliberate nod of his head. James nodded back, and Barrie saw him smile and wink at the girls. The trap was set, now all they had to do was wait, and hope Morton took the bag with him.

The barbeque turned out to be a brilliant idea and the perfect way to round the week off. Everyone was in a good mood, there was plenty of food, and each had to take it in turns to say what they'd enjoyed most about the week. Gorge walking came first overall, climbing and abseiling second, and kayaking third. The four instructors had got together and prizes were awarded to various pupils for their achievements during the week. Emily was awarded bravest climber, with Morton saying how impressed he was with her courage and determination after her scare. Jenny and Tim both got recognised for hitting the centre gold of the archery target, Miss Martin's team had won the river race and Rachel's team had won the orienteering. Medals were handed out which pupils wore round their necks proudly. The four, clapping at the appropriate times, were keeping a discreet eye on Morton throughout. He was very relaxed and after all the prizes was chatting with everyone and posing for photos.

"I've been thinking about if we do go out tonight," said Liz, having made sure no one other than the three were close enough to overhear. "Had we better make dummies for our beds so it looks like we are asleep? If someone gets up to use the toilet in the night and sees two empty bunks..." she tailed off, leaving the others to imagine what a row it would cause.

"We could put our bags under the covers, and our spare clothes," suggested Barrie. "But it might make a noise."

"How about we get a spare blanket each, roll them up and use that? It will be much easier, and they can be rolled alongside us ready. There is a cupboard in our dorm with spares in, and I expect there will be one in yours too, or you can take two from ours."

"Good thinking Jen," said Barrie. "We'll get blankets when we head in."

The evening flew by in a heartbeat and, after the food and prizes, they all joined in the toasting of marshmallows round the fire. Everyone was crowded round, holding their sticks so that the sweet treat melted and became wonderfully gooey. Tim was a little impatient with his, and held it too close. He let out an agonised yell when the marshmallow dropped off his stick, landing in the red-hot embers. Mr Atkinson, warning Tim to be more patient and careful, handed him a spare, and peace was restored.

The four were asked by Pete and Phil to regale the story of their summer adventures, having heard snippets from David. They took it in turns, as usual, and as they did, Jenny caught sight out of the corner of her eye of Ryan, sat across from the campfire pulling faces. She glared at him and, making eye contact, he stopped, but looked sullen and bad tempered.

"I wonder what it is with him," she said to herself, glad that Liz hadn't seen.

Morton was still laughing and chatting. Certainly if he was going to do what they suspected, and receive a parcel of drugs tonight, he was being super chilled. Could Liz have got the day wrong in her excitement? James wondered. Or even the week? Could it be next Thursday? He hoped not.

Barrie's sharp ears heard Miss Martin and Mr Atkinson discussing calling it a night. It was half past nine and starting to get cold, in spite of the fire. Nudging James, they moved slightly away and, taking off their coats, passed them to Jen and Liz just as Mr Atkinson stood up and announced to all that it was bedtime.

Everyone began getting up and trooping round the corner of the building to take off their boots and head into the dorms. Barrie and James hung back by the fire, they wanted to be the last in so their boots would be easy to locate later on.

Finally entering the dorm Barrie, announcing he was tired and cold, opened the cupboard to look for a blanket.

"Wouldn't be cold if you'd kept your coat on you idiot," quipped Ryan.

"Shut up, Ryan," retorted Barrie, pulling out two thick heavy blankets.

Any further spat was prevented by Mr Atkinson putting his head round the door and chivvying them into bed.

James was yawning loudly, proclaiming that he was so exhausted he could sleep for a week.

"I'll have a blanket too please, Bar," he said, and grinned as Barrie handed him it and they both made a show of being tired. No one would expect them to be up in the middle of the night.

James unplugged his phone and slid it under his duvet, then he and Barrie both got into their bunks quickly and pulled their duvets up high, so no one would notice they were still fully dressed. They quietly arranged the blankets lengthways under the duvets and hoped the girls had hidden the coats OK and were now doing similar with their blankets.

"I'll message them soon and check," thought James, as Mr Atkinson returned for lights out.

Jenny and Liz were in bed already and each had a blanket rolled up.

"Not that anything will happen," thought Jenny, gloomily, she was desperate for adventure.

With his head under his duvet, so as to not draw attention to his illuminated phone screen, James had a brief message conversation on the group chat with Liz and Jenny. The coats had been successfully hidden and the girls' boots were at the very end of the line, next to Barrie's and James'.

James checked the location of Barrie's phone; it was in the instructors' hut. He messaged the girls as much and Jenny replied that they were taking it in turns to peek through a tiny slit in the curtains towards the hut in case Morton went out without his bag.

Good idea, if nothing by midnight, we'll abandon and sleep? he replied

Yes.

OK," the girls' replied.

James set his phone alarm to vibrate every 10 minutes in case he fell asleep. He looked again at ten o'clock. Nothing.

He checked again at ten past and then at twenty past, still nothing, no movement at all.

Above him, Barrie was rather anxious about how they would manage to get his phone back in the morning if nothing happened in the night. It would take some explaining if found, and certainly he didn't want to be heading back to Grey Owls without it.

Time ticked slowly on and James felt his eyes growing heavily. A vibration jolted him awake. Eleven o'clock, no movement. He began to feel less hopeful about an adventure after all. What an anti-climax. The focus of the whole week practically had been Flittermouse Cliffs and Morton, it was very disappointing.

Ten past eleven. Nothing. James updated the girls by message and heard Barrie stirring restlessly.

Should we call it a night? Jenny, tired out, had replied.

You can stop watching if you like. I'll keep monitoring till midnight replied James.

It's OK, we'll watch till then. I think he must have meant a different Thursday. He seemed so cheery and relaxed tonight.

Yes. I think you may be right James closed his eyes waiting for the next vibration.

Twenty past. James picked up his phone to see the red dot still in the hut, but something was different. He blinked his eyes and rubbed them, refocusing them on the dot. It was in the hut, but moving. James held his breath as the dot travelled towards the door and out. Morton was on the move!

Feeling a pulse of excitement course through him, James quickly messaged Liz and Jenny and, using his feet, nudged the underside of Barrie's bunk. This was it. Time to see if their suspicions were right and their plans worked.

Both girls were highly excited, Morton had not appeared past the hostel. Jenny messaged James and he replied that Morton had gone round the other side, and was now on the path to Flittermouse Cliffs.

Quiet as mice, the girls crept from their bunks and tiptoed to the dorm door, shaking with excitement and trepidation. Just as they reached it, Liz caught her toe on a bunk leg and gave a half yelp of pain before she could stop herself. She stood, her hand over her mouth. Had anyone heard? She listened for any changes in breathing. All three were quietly sleeping. No one had heard her, and they crept out.

James and Barrie joined them in the porch as they quickly laced up their boots by a shielded light from Jen's phone

None of the four could quite believe that their guesses so far had been right and, being very careful with the door so as not to make the slightest of sounds, they crept out into the cold night air. It had dropped a few degrees even since the end of the campfire, and they all shivered, hoping it wouldn't get much colder.

Walking quickly behind the great holly tree, they went to where Liz and Jen had hidden their coats. It was a perfect hiding place and they hurriedly put them on and fastened them right up, glad of their warmth.

James checked his phone.

"Morton isn't hanging about. We'd better get moving."

They left the shelter of the holly tree and turned to head down the path and follow Morton. Barrie snuck a look back over his shoulder at the hostel, it was all in darkness.

"So far so good," he thought, jogging a few steps to catch up with the others.

But what Barrie hadn't seen in the darkness of the hostel when he had looked back, was a lone pair of eyes looking back at him. Eyes that watched the four disappear into the night. Eyes that belonged to someone determined to spoil everything.

Chapter Sixteen

A Fall in the Night

Straining his eyes in the dark, Ryan could not believe his luck! All term he had harboured a real hatred for the four and finally now, here was a fantastic opportunity to get them all into serious trouble. James and Barrie were already on warnings. Perhaps being caught sneaking off in the middle of the night would get them suspended, or even expelled. The potential made Ryan smile the widest smile he had in months; he'd spoil the perfect four's perfect time once and for all.

Ryan left the window and crossed the dorm, intent on waking Mr Atkinson. In the dim green glow of the fire exit lamp above the rear emergency door, he looked over at Barrie's and James' bunk, expecting to see the covers thrown back. Even in the low light he could see the shapes of figures under the covers. He frowned, checking his march to get the teachers mid stride. That was odd. He was sure it had been the four, though admittedly it had only been for a few seconds. That was Barrie's face he's seen in the moonlight, it had to be. But they were in bed? Ryan imagined the trouble he would get into if he woke Mr Atkinson for no reason. He crossed silently to the bunk, listening carefully for sounds of James breathing. It was silent. Too silent he thought and, his dislike of James welling up, he jabbed viciously at James' side. His straight fingers didn't hit solid torso, but sank into blankets and covers. So he had seen right, they had gone! And planned it!

"Oh," thought Ryan. "I'll get them into so much trouble." But time was passing, getting the teachers was one thing, but better surely to find out just what they were doing, then sneak back unseen and tell the teachers. That way, they couldn't come up with some stupid story.

"I bet it's a midnight feast or something," thought Ryan, excited to be spoiling their plans. "Better hurry or I will lose them," he muttered to himself, creeping to the dorm door and heading for the hostel porch.

Such was Ryan's eagerness to get out after the four that he didn't pause to change his indoor trainers for boots, or bother searching for his coat in the pile, he just closed the front door quietly and hurried out in the direction he'd seen them go.

Meanwhile, James, Jenny, Barrie and Liz were trying to walk as quickly but quietly as possible after Morton. They kept stopping every minute to check his location, Morton certainly was not hanging about, he was on a mission!

"I'm so pleased we've got your phone tracking him," panted Jenny.

"Yes. A real adventure after all! Who would have thought it after the summer?" said Liz, absolutely buzzing with excitement.

"He seems to be heading straight for Flittermouse Cliffs," said James, checking his phone. "Come on, we'll keep going but check we don't get too close. He may stop and tie a bootlace or something, we wouldn't want to fall on top of him, so keep sharp and listen out."

They continued on, straining their ears in the quiet, still night air. Quite unaware they were being followed.

Ryan felt sure he knew where the four were heading. On the first day while walking up the track to Flittermouse Cliffs, they had passed an old picnic table that was in a clearing, set back from the path. It would be the perfect place for a midnight feast. As he headed up the path, Ryan shivered and, for the first time, wished he'd brought his coat.

"I'll only be ten minutes or so," he told himself, his blue and white striped pyjamas offering little insulation against the cold October night. "One photo is all I need," he continued quietly to himself, then groaned. His phone! In Ryan's haste to get out after the four, he'd left his phone behind at the hostel, charging by his bunk.

Ryan debated what to do. Without his phone it would be just his word against theirs, but if he went back for it, he risked the four getting back too, before he could raise the alarm, or worse, he could get caught and while they got away with it. He felt momentarily sick. He had to catch them. Deciding to carry on, Ryan knew he would have to not give himself away. To secretly spy and quickly report back must be it.

It wasn't much further up the path Ryan recalled, and struck off in the dark where he thought the clearing to be. The undergrowth quickly got denser, snagging at his pyjama clad legs. Ryan cursed his haste, the torch on his phone would have prevented all this, as bramble bushes scratched at his arms. It couldn't be the way.

Struggling back to the path, Ryan hurried on. It had to be near. Just then the moon appeared from behind a cloud, illuminating the surrounding area in an eerie silvery glow.

Ryan found he was almost next to the clearing and crept slowly forward, hoping the moon would stay out long enough for him to see the four from a safe distance and dash back to tell his tale.

As he tiptoed forwards, peering round a wide tree trunk, the moonlight lit up the clearing, with its old table. It was completely deserted. Ryan couldn't believe it. He scanned all round and crossed to the table, looking for signs the four had been there, crumbs left on the table, anything. There was nothing.

Had they slipped back past him while he was getting tangled and scratched by the briars? It would be dreadful if they had and he was the one caught out of bounds in the dead of night. Ryan stood, shivering on the path, wondering what to do next and trying to stop the panic rising. He had almost decided to head back to the hostel when he heard the sound of an owl, hooting mournfully and again. Didn't Jenny often hoot like an owl? Was it her playing a game with the other three? Decision made, Ryan marched on, positive the four must be just ahead of him.

As the four continued to track Morton a tawny owl hooted, and was immediately answered by another, surprisingly near. James jumped slightly.

"Spooky," said Jenny, squeezing Liz's hand and fighting the urge to hoot back.

On they went. They couldn't quite match Morton's pace whilst being careful and quiet, but were confident Barrie's phone would keep them on the right track.

"Do you know something?" said Liz, in a low voice to Jenny, "I can't help but feel like we're being followed. You don't think Morton is with anyone do you, and they're following up behind?"

"I doubt it," whispered back Jenny, but all the same she nudged Barrie and James, "Liz thinks we're being followed."

"It's just a feeling," said Liz.

"I bet it's because of that owl," said James, reassuringly. "It's spooked you and got you imagining things. If Morton had someone, they'd be with him, not way behind, and if it was who he was meeting, they'd meet nearer to the hostel. No point walking all this way if you are walking the same path."

A sudden rustle in the undergrowth near them made them all freeze abruptly. What was that? It sounded large and powerful, and seemed to be moving quite quickly towards them. Was it someone lying in wait for Morton to return? Or to meet him? In an instant, Jenny's overactive imagination had conjured up all sorts of terrifying beasts and she clung to Liz in fright. Feeling highly alarmed, Liz and Jenny both snapped their torches on, and shone them in the direction of the sound, expecting to see, they didn't know what.

In the beam of their torches a black and white wedge-shaped head with beady black eyes looked back at them, unblinking. It stood motionless for a second, before turning and running back through the undergrowth with impressive speed, quickly disappearing out of sight.

"Heavens to Betsy! It's a badger." Liz made to follow it. She'd never seen a badger in real life before and automatically wanted to see more of it.

"Liz! No!" hissed James after her, worried that Morton would hear her crashing about in the trees. Liz checked her headlong flight; her desire to follow the badger surpassed only by her desire to discover what Morton's secret was. Turning, she shone her way back to the other three, wondering just what else was moving around at night.

Ryan, meanwhile, had been walking as quickly as he could. The clouds had passed in front of the moon again, blotting out most of the light, which slowed Ryan considerably. He couldn't afford to step off the track. It was right next to the gorge in places and one foot wrong could send him plunging down into the icy water. In the darkness, through the trees some way ahead, he saw a brief flash of a torch. It was only for a second, but he felt sure it must be the four and grinned, hurrying after them as quickly as he could.

The four, their panic at the sound of the badger over, carried on, glad of their torches when the moon disappeared. They shielded them well, and only used them when absolutely necessary, unsure what else and who else was about.

"I still have the feeling that someone's behind us," said Liz, after a few minutes of silent walking.

"It's just because you got spooked," repeated James. "First by the owl, then the badger. Don't worry. There's no one following us. I'm sure of it."

But Liz's feeling was right. Ryan was indeed following them, catching the odd glimpse of them in the moonlight. He was getting closer.

Looking at his phone, James updated everyone. "Morton has just entered the wooded section. We can slow down as we will be noisy going through the trees, especially with the fallen branches. Better let him get well clear."

Pausing and catching their breath, all eyes were on James' phone screen.

"Flittermouse Cliffs is about there," pointed James, as the red dot moved steadily towards it. "As soon as he's clear of the woods, we'll get going again." He frowned suddenly in the dark. "Hang on, he's changing direction!"

"Not coming back is he?" asked Liz, immediately looking round for somewhere to hide.

They all peered earnestly at the screen.

"No, he's turned inland, away from the gorge up the steep embankment."

"So he's not going to Flittermouse Cliffs after all?" asked Barrie, disappointed.

"Doesn't look so," said James, showing Barrie the screen more closely.

"I think that embankment turns into a bit of a rough crag, like a wall of huge boulders," said Liz, who'd taken much interest in the woods on the two previous occasions.

"So where on earth is he off to?" wondered Barrie, out loud. "And where will it take him?"

"I think he'll come out above the cliffs," said James. "We'll wait till he's at the top, or he may spot us from being a bit higher up. Once he's at the top, all the trees will hide us."

They watched the red dot travel slowly across the screen as Morton climbed up the crag.

"Hope we don't need ropes," muttered Barrie.

"We'll have a go," said James. "Come on, he's at the top."

They all hurried along and soon were in the woods. It was tricky and they were pretty much feeling their way along, wanting to keep torch use to an absolute minimum.

The sound of twigs snapping under their feet, like small gun shots, and the odd muffled exclamation as a shin hit a branch or a limb of a fallen tree made them all realise just how right they had been to wait for Morton to exit the wooded area.

"Much louder and we'd wake the dead," remarked James, as a dark mass loomed up in front of them.

At the foot of the crag they all carefully shone their torches at the stoney face. Huge moss-covered rocks and boulders were piled up like a rockery in a fairy-tale giant's garden.

"Go careful," said James. "Carry your torches in your teeth so you can use both hands." Both the girls and James had torches which they'd bought in Wales. Barrie had chosen to buy a head torch, leaving his hands free for climbing more easily, so he led the way.

It was treacherous and hard work. Even in the cold October night air the children were sweating in their coats, the boulders were large with few places obvious in the dark to get hold of to pull yourself up.

Jenny slipped on moss and landed heavily on her knee. She made a face with the pain, biting her lip to stop from crying out.

James had heard her slip.

"Are you OK, Jen?" he whispered, from just above her.

"I'll have a killer bruise, but I'm OK," replied Jenny, rubbing her painful knee.

It was as she sat for a moment, waiting for the pain in her knee to subside, that Jenny distinctly heard someone below the four. The sound of a twig snapping carried up, and from not very far away. Jenny felt the hairs on the back of her neck stand up.

"There's someone following," whispered Jenny, quietly to James, switching off her torch. James immediately passed the message on to Barrie and Liz up ahead.

Everyone froze and snapped off their torches. Yes. In the dark there was the sound of someone moving in the woods below them. The footfalls were not that of anything like a badger. Whoever it was, was moving slowly and deliberately, trying to be quiet. As the four sat, not daring to breathe, and listening in the pitch dark as hard as they could, they heard the unmistakable sound of someone slowly climbing up the crag after them.

Shaking with fear, and unable to stand it any longer, Jenny pointed her torch towards the sound and snapped it on. She let out an exclamation.

"Ryan!"

Ryan, wide eyed in his pyjamas, looked directly into the light of the torch and went to climb higher. His left foot pressed onto a patch of moss and the four watched in horror as he slipped. There was a brief scream as Ryan fell backward off the crag, landing on the ground below with a dull thud.

Chapter Seventeen

The Four are Divided

A low moan from the bottom of the crag told the four Ryan was conscious.

"Jenny, your owl noise," suggested James, and immediately Jenny produced a series of tawny owl calls. If Morton had heard the scream from Ryan, he may think it was an owl screech.

The four all quickly and carefully clambered down to where Ryan lay. Seeing where he had slipped, Ryan had actually only fallen a few feet, but had landed awkwardly. He was holding his ankle and looked quite pale in the torchlight.

"Are you OK?" asked Jenny, reaching him first

"What do you care?" answered Ryan, before letting out a whimper.

"Is it just your ankle?" asked James, resisting the urge to ask Ryan what the hell he was doing following them in his pyjamas in the middle of the night.

"I think so," answered Ryan, a little more civilly.

"Well, this ruins everything," said Barrie. "How can we track Morton and possibly find the drugs? We have Ryan to take care of."

Ryan looked rather taken aback, at the mention of Morton and drugs. He'd thought they were just messing about, and had never for a moment thought they may be mixed up in an actual adventure.

There was a moment's silence, as they all considered just how close they were to possibly discovering a huge secret. It seemed absolutely typical that, of all the people to put an end to their adventure, it would be Ryan, and it was so frustrating after all their efforts.

"Doesn't take all four of us," said Liz her voice low and urgent. "Two stay with Ryan and two follow Morton as best as you can. But we need to decide quickly before it's too late and he's too far ahead."

"I'd better follow as my phone is tracking," said James.

Jenny glanced at Liz, who was looking uncomfortably at Ryan.

"You go Liz," she said, generously, knowing how hurt Liz had been and how much she'd not want to be left with him.

"Right. Better not move him till we're back. Then we'll get him back to the hostel somehow," said James, taking off his coat. "Here, he'll need this to get warm. I'll be OK without, I'm moving."

Barrie took the offered coat and draped it round Ryan's shoulders as James and Liz turned to scramble carefully back up the crag.

Accompanied by hushed calls of "Good luck!" James and Liz gingerly reclimbed the crag, moving carefully from boulder to boulder, acutely aware that one wrong move could send them tumbling down to the three below. They reached the top and James checked his phone.

"He's gone left, towards Flittermouse Cliffs and is stationary. Wonder if we've missed the meet. No, wait, he's moving again. He's going away from the cliffs now, inland, and he's really moving quite quickly."

They hurried on, jogging a little in parts when the moonlight allowed. Morton seemed to be crossing a field, walking quickly.

As they reached the point where Morton had paused, they carefully shone their torches about. Liz's beam fell on a blue climbing rope, coiled on the floor. It was dry, whereas the ground was damp, so hadn't been there long.

"Odd," said James. "Why dump that? And why carry it all this way for nothing? Anyway, come on, he looks to be on a track between a field and some woods."

Turning inland, using only the moonlight to see by, James and Liz hurried on, this was all very strange, but exciting too.

They couldn't guess where Morton would lead them, but were determined to follow him wherever he went. Liz, panting with the effort of walking at such a pace, looked quickly at her phone for the time.

"We've been going for over half an hour," she whispered. "Can't be much further, it's nearly midnight."

"No," agreed James. "He must surely be nearly there, if the meeting is still at midnight. I have no idea where there is though, we seem to be in the middle of nowhere."

"Do you think we should call the police?" asked Liz. "It'll take them ages to get here, we are miles from anywhere."

"What would we tell them?" asked James, his mind automatically thinking of the facts as opposed to their suspicions and theories. "An instructor is out in the middle of the night and may, or may not be meeting someone for drugs. With only a part of a one-sided phone call overheard to give us that thought. I reckon they'd see it as a wind up and ignore us. Dad says people are often ringing in for silly reasons, like asking for bus times or complaining a pizza shop is shut." He paused, thinking more. "I wish we'd thought to buy a copy of the paper, or even just search the local news online. I didn't think."

"I should have bought a paper, but I was in such a tearing hurry to tell you all, I didn't think and actually, I don't think I had enough money anyway."

"It doesn't matter," said James, "but we'll not call until we actually see what he is up to."

"Ok. I hope whatever it is, is soon. I've got a stitch and my legs are really starting to ache."

They could see the silhouette of the woods looming up and slowed. James checked his phone. Morton was stationary, about halfway down the track just where it forked to go across the next field. He zoomed out, the track looked to be just a farm access track to fields, if they continued on for about half a mile, they'd reach a road. He showed the phone to Liz.

"We'll get as close as we dare, but have to be absolutely silent," he whispered.

Liz nodded. "Is your phone on silent?" she asked. The last thing they needed was a message from Jenny making a noise, James checked, it was.

Holding their breath and walking almost on tip toes, the pair crept along until they were only about 30 metres from Morton. They couldn't see him and dared not get any closer. Now they had to wait and see who turned up. They stood silently, every fibre of their being on edge. What would happen?

Jenny and Barrie meanwhile were doing their best to make Ryan comfortable.

"We'll get you back as soon as James and Liz are back, and I don't think that will be long," said Barrie, trying to reassure Ryan and hoping the other two wouldn't be away too long.

Ryan grunted a reply. He had manoeuvred himself to a more comfortable position, sitting on the ground with his injured ankle now elevated on a low rock which Jenny had put under it.

Barrie had helped Ryan put James' coat on properly, and had offered his own too.

Jenny looked at Ryan in James' coat, which was too big for him. In the torchlight he looked much younger than his twelve years, with his surly attitude gone, he looked more like ten.

She shone her torch on his ankle, it was swelling, and she knew from when she'd hurt her wrist years ago that cold helped.

"Cold is good for injuries to limbs. I can put my jumper in cold water, then put it on your ankle. It will help."

Before Barrie could protest, Jenny stood up and began heading off towards the gorge.

"Be careful!" he called after her, in a low tone.

Jenny was careful, and at the edge of the wood, she quickly removed her coat and jumped, putting her coat back on before dropping onto her front on the bank of the gorge. Fortunately, the bank dipped low there and, by holding onto one sleeve, she could dangle most of the jumper in the ice flow. Jenny changed sleeves so all the jumper was soaked and then hauled it onto the bank; it was quite a lot heavier now.

Trying hard to get wet as little as possible, Jenny retraced her steps back to Barrie and Ryan.

"Here, this will help," she said, wrapping the cold wet jumper round Ryan's swollen ankle. Barrie, she saw, had taken off his jumper and laid it over Ryan's pyjama clad legs.

"How's that?" she asked, tying the sleeves gently round the bottom of Ryan's leg.

When Ryan didn't reply, she shone her torch on his face. Tears were rolling down his cheeks.

"Oh, no. Is it hurting more?" she asked, wondering if her makeshift bandage was too tight.

Ryan shook his head. He tried to speak but only gut wrenching sobs came out.

"Hey," said Jenny, instinctively putting an arm round him. Barrie squatted down by him.

"What is it?" he asked, his sky blue eyes full of concern.

Ryan tried to control his sobbing. "Why are you looking after me?" he asked, in between sobs. "Why are you being kind?"

"You're hurt," replied Jenny.

"Yes. You need our help," added Barrie. "We won't leave you."

"But I've been horrible to you all term," said Ryan, his sobs increasing as large tears continued to roll down his blotchy cheeks. I followed you here to get you into trouble. Ever since summer I've hated you."

"We did kind of get that impression," said Jenny, not feeling it was the time to be reproachful.

"I'm sorry," said Ryan, breaking down again, his shoulders shaking up and down as he cried.

"Dad says everyone acts for a reason," said Barrie, who had often wondered just why Ryan had turned from being someone they barely knew in the first year, to the boy who tried everything to make their lives miserable.

"I'm sorry," repeated Ryan, as even more tears burst out, "I'm so, so sorry."

Jenny and Barrie let him cry and, as he again gathered himself, Ryan continued.

"You see when you were having your amazing summer, I was having my worst. You had all the fun, the fame and excitement. I had endless rows and shouting at home. It was awful. Mum and Dad were arguing all the time. The week before terms started, they told me they were getting divorced. It's awful. I hated you for having all the happiness I'd lost. Every mention of your adventure in the summer, just reminded me of my summer and how everything is just so horrible at home."

It all started to make sense now. The online comments, the note, the name calling. Ryan was lashing out at the four because they had what he wanted, happiness.

"It'll be OK," said Jenny. "Different, but OK."

Ryan slowly quietened down, it seemed all his fight was gone and he was just a hurt, vulnerable boy. Jenny, looking at his forlorn figure, couldn't believe they had been made so upset by him. At least now they knew why.

"It will help Liz knowing why Ryan acted like he did," she thought, and then looking at Barrie said "I wonder how Liz and James are getting on.

Half a mile away from Jenny, James and Liz stood silently in the woods just off the track. Every nerve was on edge, every sense seemed heightened as they strained to see or hear any movement in the dark.

Liz slipped her hand into James', a reassuring squeeze from him she felt stopped her heart jumping out of her chest just in time.

They heard the odd twig crack a little further along in the direction Barrie's phone had gone. Morton was moving a little.

"Impatiently waiting," thought James, well at least it told them where he was.

Aside from the twigs snapping, the only sounds to punctuate the still, silent night were the 'kerwick' and 'twoo' of tawny owls and the distant shrill bark of a fox. It was eerily quiet, as if the whole place was waiting for something.

That wait was soon over.

A car could be heard approaching down the track, coming from the direction of the road. James leaned out of the tree line, he could definitely hear a car moving slowly along, but couldn't see one. The moonlight dimly picked out a large shape some distance away.

"No lights," he whispered in Liz's ear.

The hairs on the back of James' neck were stood up on end, and Liz had butterflies in her stomach.

Both peeking out from the woods, they saw a sudden glow of red for a moment.

"Brake lights," said James.

The engine tone changed and a white glow appeared to one side.

"They're turning round in the fork," continued James.

"I hope they're not just lost," said Liz, who felt she just couldn't bear such an anticlimax.

"No, they'd have lights on if they were just lost. Whoever this is, they're up to no good alright." He smiled in the dark, it was a phrase his dad used sometimes when talking about the villains he'd caught.

"Heavens to Betsy," breathed Liz.

Brake lights shone again, but this time they were facing James and Liz, the car had turned round to face back towards the road. The sound of the engine died.

A passenger door opened, activating the interior light.

"Two?" asked Liz, seeing the outline of two people in the car.

"Yes, I think so," confirmed James. "Let's get closer."

Holding hands still, they crept forward. Ahead they could hear more movement from the woods and, as the moon appeared from behind a cloud, they could see a dark figure emerge from the woods right by the car. A torch flashed briefly at the figure from the car, yes, it was Morton who had come out of the woods.

Seeing it was who they were expecting, two males got out of the car, and all three stood near the boot.

"Can't be too careful, bit more activity around," said a voice James and Liz didn't recognise.

"No one for miles," said Morton in a low voice. "And you're sure this is good stuff? None of that muck you sold me last week? I don't want people getting hurt."

One of the men snorted, as if he didn't care whether people got hurt or not.

"It's good, I promise," said the other. "You have the money?"

There was the sound of Morton delving into his pocket and, in the light of the man's torch, he produced a wad of notes.

The light also illuminated the car's number plate and James whispered it. They'd need that for the police.

He quickly opened the camera function on his phone, that might get it.

"No flash!" hissed Liz, urgently.

James checked himself, his finger hovering over the capture icon. It was set to auto flash.

"Ta," he said, pressing the screen to turn the flash off and selecting night mode.

Silently he zoomed in and he got several photos of the three by the rear of the car. It hadn't got all the number plate, but he could remember the first two it missed, TN.

The boot of the car was opened, the number plate on the tailgate disappearing from view. An interior light in the boot shone and all three men looked inside.

"All yours," said the driver, a white man with dark hair and a few days' stubble. Morton took his rucksack from his back and began to fiddle with the opening.

"Not the top pocket, not the top pocket!" willed both James and Liz. If the phone was discovered now, it would be a disaster.

Packages were carefully lifted by Morton and placed in his bag.

"Time to call the police?" suggested Liz.

"Yes, I'll ring them. Can you try and video what you can while I do?"

She nodded and James disappeared quickly and quietly into the woods.

Leaving Liz capturing all she could on video, as soon as he felt he was far enough away, James dialled 999.

"Which emergency service do you require?" said a voice almost immediately.

"Police, please," said James.

"Connecting you now."

A few seconds later a female voice came on the line.

"What is your emergency?"

James gabbled the vehicle registration while he could remember it and quickly told of his feeling that there was a drug deal going on, a car with no lights in a lonely place, an overheard conversation and mysterious midnight meets.

"How old are you, son?" asked the call taker.

"Twelve. But you have to believe me. My dad is Sergeant Russell in Newcastle. This isn't a prank, I swear."

There was a pause as the vehicle, and possibly his father's details were being checked through. It was agonising for James. What if the police didn't believe him and wouldn't come out?

"What is the exact location?" asked the voice, sounding serious.

James described it from his map.

"I'm sending someone to you now."

"If they hear sirens, they'll scarper," said James, imagining blue lights and sirens wailing across the quiet night air. The noise would carry for miles.

I'm dispatching a plain vehicle. It will not have lights on," said the call taker, taking some more details from James. He couldn't describe the men much, other than both being white and unshaven. One had dark hair, the other had a beanie hat on. He wished he could say more about them, but it was too dark. The call taker seemed pleased with what he had remembered though, noting it all down.

"I can stay on the line with you until they arrive," offered the call taker reassuringly.

"No thanks, I need to get back to my friend."

"Ok, I have got your number. The officers will ring you if they need to when they're near. Do not approach the males and do not take any risks. If anything else happens or you feel in danger, phone 999 immediately."

"I will. Thank you," said James, ending the call. He had to get back to Liz.

Reaching her, she was still filming. Hearing James' approach, she turned.

"Six packages."

"Police are coming," said James. "But," he continued, as the two men shut the boot and got back into their car, "will they make it in time?"

Chapter Eighteen

A Desperate Race

As Liz and James watched, the two men got into their car. The engine started up and, still without lights on, the car drove away down the track towards the road.

"The police might pick them up," whispered James. "I gave them the vehicle registration number."

Liz suddenly pulled his sleeve urgently, taking them both further into the woods. She'd spotted Morton turning to come back along the track and realised they'd be easily seen, right on the edge of the trees.

The pair held their breath as Morton passed by them. Still carrying the rucksack, he was walking purposefully back in the direction they'd come from, back towards the cliffs and gorge.

"We should warn Jen and Bar," suggested Liz. "If Morton goes down the crag, he'll land straight on them."

"Yes, send a quick message then let's get after Morton."

Liz typed in the group chat:

M on way back. If can, get away from crag.

"Right, let's go!" said Liz, pocketing her phone.

James checked his phone; Morton was still on the track. He and Liz set off after him. Fortunately, the moon was quite bright and the clouds had cleared, so they could easily walk quickly without fear of tripping.

"Does mean we are easier to spot," commented James, quietly.

"Good point," said Liz, and slowed her pace slightly. "Bar's phone is doing the hard work for us."

"Yes," said James. "I hope the police get here soon,"

OK flashed up on James' phone from the group chat.

"Jen's got your message," said James.

Jenny had read the message out to Barrie. "We'll need to move you if you think you can?" he said to Ryan.

"It's only my ankle," said Ryan. "If you can pull me up?"

Barrie and Jenny each held an outstretched arm of Ryan's and heaved him up to his feet. With all his weight on his good leg, and leaning heavily on Barrie, he tested his hurt ankle, gingerly putting some weight on it.

Wincing with pain, Ryan declared that he could walk a bit with help and together, the three made slow progress along the crag face to a steep section where they stopped at the base.

"We should be able to safely see if he comes this way," said Barrie, looking to where they'd been sitting.

Both Jenny and Barrie were desperate to know what was going on for Liz and James, but knew they'd have to be patient. Any unnecessary messaging now could spoil everything. They had told Ryan all about their suspicions. About Liz overhearing Morton's phone call and the concern that there were dangerous drugs, about to do serious harm to people. Ryan sat dumbfounded. He could hardly believe that, while being regular kids on a half term trip, the four of them had managed to uncover such a mystery, and he'd nearly ruined it. Ryan felt even more ashamed of his behaviour. The four should be admired, not despised. It wasn't their fault his parents were splitting up. He didn't know how he would put all his wrongs right, but he felt determined to try, if they'd let him.

Up at the top, Morton had walked quickly back across the field, the way he had come. When he got to the edge of the field though, he turned right, away from the crag and onto the cliff top path towards Flittermouse Cliffs.

James and Liz kept pace. Pausing at where the rope had been abandoned, Liz risked a second's flash with her torch.

"Rope's gone," she said.

"If he's going somewhere you need rope for, we've no hope of following him. Oh where are the police?" Looking at his phone, James added, "He's stopped. Right at the top of Flittermouse Cliffs."

Just as they both looked at his phone the screen lit up with an incoming call flashing from a private number.

"This has to be the police," said James, answering. "Hello?"

"Hello, is this James? It's PC Leedal and PC Murphy, Northumbria Police. We have come to the location you told our control room about, but there's no one here."

"The car drove off, not long after I put the phone down to your lot," said James. "But the man who took all the packages is on foot. He's walking now and we've been following him."

"Are we to continue down the track you told us to get to?" asked the officer, impressed at James' tracking of the man.

"Yes. We've gone further down the track, across a field and along a cliff top path," explained James, quietly, "We're still following him."

"We're now at the end of the track. Which way from here?" asked the officer and James had an idea

"I'll share my location with you if you can give me your mobile number."

"Excellent," said the officer and passed his number. James added it as a contact and quickly shared his location.

"Our vehicle is four-wheel drive; we'll get as far as we can in it and then the rest on foot. Be with you as soon as possible."

Ending the call, James checked the location of Barrie's phone again. It hadn't moved and was still at the top of Flittermouse Cliffs.

The dot then seemed to waiver, and moved to the edge of the cliff, jumping between that and the path at the bottom, alongside the gorge.

"Do you think he's found Bar's phone and thrown it over the cliff edge?" asked Liz, watching the red dot dance on the screen.

"No, I reckon he's going down the cliff and the GPS is trying to make sense," said James.

There was the sound of running footsteps. James and Liz immediately looked towards the sound. Was this the police or yet another midnight wanderer? They both stood alert, poised and ready to run if it was trouble.

James flashed his torch and could see a man and woman were quickly approaching. They were both dressed in dark clothing and didn't look like police officers.

"Get ready to run," he whispered to Liz as the pair slowed.

"James?" asked the male, and James recognised his voice from the call. It was the police officer, and now that they were close, he could see their stab vests, bulky under their coats, the antenna from their radios sticking out.

Two warrant cards, similar to his father's were shown to James and Liz.

"I'm PC Leedal, Tony, and this is PC Murphy, Kate. "Where's our man with the bag?" asked Tony, urgently, and James showed his screen.

"You're tracking him on your phone!" exclaimed Tony. "How the..." he stopped his questions knowing they needed to act fast. There would be plenty of time for questions later.

"This way," said James, gesturing along the path, and the four now set off as a group in hot pursuit.

It was comforting having the two plain clothed police officers with them. All the pressure James had felt on his shoulders was much less. Help was here, and everything would be alright surely. Soon they passed the section they'd climbed up and a short distance ahead was where they'd abseiled. They passed that point and, after a few dozen paces, James stopped.

"Here," he whispered.

"There's no one here," said Kate, and shone her torch. The path was empty and deserted. James and Liz immediately began looking round for Barrie's phone, or the bag. Anything that would help show where Morton now was.

A movement where part of the cliff jutted up caught Liz's eye.

"Look," she said, flashing her torch in that direction.

There, looped through an eye bolt, was a blue climbing rope. The two officers immediately inspected the rope.

"He's making his escape down the cliff," said Tony, very clever, very clever indeed. Our man is no amateur.

"Can we stop him?" asked James. "Grab the rope or pull it back up?"

"No," said Tony. "We don't know what it's fastened to, and if anything was to go wrong, it could be a real disaster. Imagine if he fell down the cliff. You're not going to survive a fall from this height."

Liz and James both felt sick. They'd liked Morton and didn't want him getting hurt, even if he was a bad lot.

Tony looked frustrated. "He'll be down at the bottom and gone in no time."

"He's an instructor at the youth hostel. Can we not head there?" asked Liz.

"He may not return there," said Tony. "We need to get him now, before he has a chance to offload the stuff and come up with a story."

"We can't follow him down on the rope?" asked James, determined that they should reach Morton.

Again, Tony shook his head. "We've no harnesses." He paused, considering the matter. "We could go to our vehicle, drive to the hostel, but I don't hold much hope of your man having a bag full of drugs. He's likely going to head elsewhere, possibly meeting buyers. He'd be crazy to take a bag of drugs into a hostel."

"He did say this week was the last week of the season," said James.

"My bet is he's not going to go back there at all," said Kate, something none of the children had considered. "He'll disappear with his haul, sell it all over winter and then pop up elsewhere, different county, different country. If we don't catch him now, there's a chance we never will."

"At least though we can track him on my phone." Illuminating the screen again to show the red dot James let out a cry of dismay. "Low battery! I can't believe it, it was full!"

Continually tracking and refreshing was using a lot of power and, although it had been fully charged at half past nine last night, it wouldn't be able to track for much longer.

"The rope's moving," said Liz, pointing to the eye bolt. The rope had begun to slide through and, as they watched, transfixed, the end of the rope appeared, passed through the eye bolt and dropped down the cliff face.

"What's the quickest way down?" asked Kate, her voice urgent.

"We came up by the crags, it's the only way we know," said James.

"Let's go," said Tony. "If we hurry, and he goes back that way, we may just be able to catch him up. If not, then he's won, and if he doesn't return to the hostel, as Kate says, we may never get him."

They headed off as fast as they could along the cliff path, four beams of torchlight illuminating the way, but they knew that Morton had a much easier, faster and more direct route.

"We need to delay him," thought Liz. "Slow him down."

Pulling out her phone, to the police officers surprise, she rang Jenny as she half walked and half jogged.

"Morton's on his way from the bottom of Flittermouse Cliffs. We're with the police heading to come down the crag. Can you delay him somehow? Say you've been out looking for owls and got lost or something?"

James explained to Tony and Kate that Jenny and Barrie were at the bottom of the crag.

"How many of you are there, roaming about in the night, looking for criminals?" asked Kate, bemused. She had never met any kids like these before.

"Four, well, five, but Ryan wasn't meant to be here. He's hurt his ankle and is in pyjamas, and my coat," panted James.

Tony shook his head; this would take some working out.

"They're going to try," said Liz, ending the call.

Jenny had put the phone on speakerphone, so Barrie and Ryan had heard everything.

"I don't want to leave Ryan," said Barrie, worried about him being hurt. "We should stick together."

Ryan, deeply ashamed about how he'd wanted to, and almost succeeded in, ruining everything, wanted to do anything he could to help.

"If you can help me hobble down to the track, I can cry out and Morton will have to help us. I can make a fuss so he feels he has to stay. Please let me help. I feel so bad. I want to try for you."

"I don't know," said Barrie. "What if Morton turns nasty and you can't get away?"

"You said Liz said he was angry at people getting hurt. I don't think he's going to hurt me, and really, it's our best chance. Please let me try?" begged Ryan.

"It's worth a go," said Jenny, and Barrie reluctantly nodded. Jenny and Barrie helped Ryan to his feet and they headed off to intercept Morton as James, Liz and the two police officers hurried to meet them.

Getting to the edge of the track, where the path coming from the hostel entered the wooded section, Ryan was helped to sit on a fallen tree trunk. Jenny and Barrie waited nervously, scanning the trees for any sign of movement.

Twigs snapping alerted them, but was it Morton or the police? A dark figure approached and Ryan let out a groan. The figure stopped immediately and a torch was switched on.

"Ryan!" said Morton, in a surprised voice, "What on earth?"

Jenny and Barrie looked, Morton had his rucksack on his back and a blue climbing rope slung over his shoulder.

"Ryan has fallen over this log," said Jenny. "His ankle..." she pointed. "We got lost. We came to search for owls and bats you see..." she hoped Morton wouldn't guess they'd been following him.

"Let me look," said Morton, crouching down by Ryan's ankle. It was swollen and Ryan yelped and screwed up his face as the jumper was removed, making out it was very painful indeed.

"Where are the other two?" asked Morton. "And why are you in your pyjamas, Ryan? Honestly, this place is dangerous in the dark, I'll have to go and get help."

"Don't leave me," wailed Ryan, clutching at Morton's arm. "I'm scared." He clung to Morton's arm like a drowning man would cling to a life ring. Jenny and Barrie were impressed, he was certainly very convincing.

"The other two went to try and get help," said Jenny, trying to put Morton off leaving. "I'm sure they'll be back soon, with David hopefully. They were going to try him before the teachers. I mean, you and him, but you're here." Jenny hoped Morton hadn't picked up on her slip that they'd known he wasn't at the hut. He didn't seem to.

Barrie kept glancing towards the crag. He didn't think they'd be able to delay Morton much longer, who was gently feeling Ryan's ankle, reassuring him that he didn't think it was broken.

Ryan kept wailing and grabbing at Morton, hoping the noise he was making would help the others and police find them quickly. Morton tried his best to soothe him and patiently explained that the sooner he went, the sooner they'd have help.

He was just gently prizing Ryan's hand from his coat sleeve when torch lights appeared and shouts from James and Liz made him pause as they ran through the woods.

When the police came into view just behind James and Liz, Morton's first thought was that they had rung the police for help for Ryan. He quickly realised otherwise, but it was too late when, to his surprise, Tony swiftly took hold of his bag and informed him under the Misuse of Drugs Act, it would be searched.

"Go ahead," said Morton, completely nonchalantly. "But there's an injured boy here."

Kate crossed to Ryan, who'd stopped his commotion and was sitting quietly, wide eyed.

"Help is coming," she said, as Tony opened the bag.

Seven pairs of eyes watched as Tony emptied the bag of its entire contents.

The four held their breath as map booklets, Barrie's phone, which he quickly retrieved, a small first aid kit, some climbing nuts and carabiners were all laid out by the bag. Tony shook the bag, and patted it down thoroughly, in case there were any hidden compartments. He put it down.

One thing was very apparent to all there.. There were no packages.

Chapter Nineteen

Barrie Solves the Secret

James and Liz stared at the bag's contents open-mouthed.

"But there were six packages!" blurted Liz, feeling quite incredulous.

Morton looked momentarily shocked at Liz's mention of six packages, Jenny noticed, but he said nothing.

Tony looked at the bag, and back at the children. He'd been pranked by kids before, but something about James and Liz had impressed him, and despite the bag being empty, he felt they were genuine. At worst, it was a misplaced call with good intent, he thought.

"They could be anywhere now," he said, struggling to keep the frustration from his voice. "It's a good way from where you rang us from. I'll have to call out the drugs dog. He might be our best chance of finding them."

"A drugs dog?" laughed Morton. "What on earth have these kids been telling you. Honestly, officer, get a dog, it won't find anything, there's nothing to find. I think too much excitement at the barbeque last night has addled their brains." Certainly, if Morton had just received a shipment of drugs, he was playing it as cool as ice, acting bemused.

"Should you not be more bothered about Ryan here?"

Tony moved a short distance away, leaving Kate with Morton, so he could use his radio discreetly.

He returned after a few minutes.

"A dog is on its way. It is a good few miles away so it will take a bit of time, so we'll have to sit tight."

The four studied Morton as this news was shared. He didn't seem in the least bit concerned. Panic began to rise in all four of them. Had they got this spectacularly wrong and accused an innocent man of being a drug dealing criminal? It was true that Morton had always been nice and friendly, but then Barrie had felt there was something at the start of the week, and there had to be something in what Liz had overheard, yet here he was as cool as a cucumber.

James took the opportunity of taking Barrie out of earshot and updating him quickly about what had gone on, the hike over the fields to the track, the waiting in some woods, before a car arriving with no lights on.

Barrie's eyes were open wide at James and Liz actually seeing the exchange, and then Morton going over the cliffs. He was sorry he'd missed that part of the excitement. As he thought about what James and Liz had seen, and the journey back, a bell started ringing in his mind, that bell grew louder and he saw everything falling into place.

"I know where the drugs are, I know where the drugs are!" he said excitedly, his words tumbling over themselves in his hurry to get them out. "There has to be a reason Morton abseiled down rather than use the crags. It's genius!"

"I'd thought for speed and safety," admitted James. "It was very tricky coming down the crag in the dark, even with the torches. If you could slide down the cliff effortlessly and avoid risking breaking an ankle or worse..."

"He's abseiled. And is showing absolutely no concern about a drugs dog searching the path between the exchange and here," continued Barrie. "Think about it. Why isn't he bothered about the dog?"

James looked at Barrie, his eyes widening as what Barrie had worked out dawned on him also.

"The drugs are hidden in the crevice in the cliffs. The one he said was used by bats!" finished Barrie, looking triumphant. "There's no way a drugs dog would ever find them and, whenever he needs to get some for a buyer, he just climbs up and gets them, like he did that night I accidentally left my phone in his bag. It's genius!" he repeated.

"We need to tell Tony," said James and they went quickly over to where the officer was talking into his radio.

"Excuse me," said James, and Tony turned, "Barrie knows where the drugs are and a dog is going to be no use at all."

Tony took them further away to have more privacy.

"Go on," said Tony, doubtfully, how could this boy, who'd not even been with them know where the drugs were. If this was an elaborate wind up, Tony would be the laughing stock of the station, and would throw the book at the kids.

Barrie quickly explained and Tony, listening carefully, nodded.

"It's possible," he said, and got back onto his radio.

The boys waited. How would they get the drugs out of the cliff at half past midnight?

A few moments later, Tony turned to the boys.

"Right. I've another unit coming to help. We're lucky. Another member of our team, Dan, is an experienced climber and does a lot in his spare time. He's popping back to the station to get his harness and ropes and stuff from his car, then he'll meet us at the cliff top and we'll see if your theory is right. I've got MRT coming to get the lad in the pyjamas out of here too. They shouldn't take too long and it might be easier for them to get him up the cliff than us stretcher him all the way down the path to the hostel."

"MRT?" asked James.

"Mountain rescue team," explained Tony. "And our control room knows I've five of you here with me, so a unit is going to the hostel to let the teachers know you're safe and well. The last thing we want is you being discovered missing and everybody panicking."

"Oh hell," said James, imagining the look of fury that would be on Miss Martin's face when she was woken by the police. "There had better be drugs, or we're for the high jump."

More hushed discussions were had between Tony and Kate. Morton was not allowed to leave and had no idea that anyone was coming to climb down the cliff. Still thinking they were waiting for a drugs dog, he sat quietly with Ryan whom he had already put his coat over, and a space blanket from the first aid kit in his bag. Looking at the way he was caring for Ryan, neither Liz nor Jenny, stood a little away so they could watch everything, could believe he was into drugs.

"Right," said Tony, beckoning the four children to him. "Dan is going to abseil down the cliffs where Morton did. I just need one of you kids to show from the bottom where Dan is to look. Who can help with that?" he looked at Barrie.

Barrie knew none of the four could bear to not be there at the end. Either way, this would finish the adventure. Packages and victory, or nothing and frustration, likely coupled with detention for life!

"We'd all come please," said Barrie. "We four stick together, you see."

"I want to come too," said a small voice, Ryan had stood up and managed to hobble over to them, not wanting to miss out. He'd just caught the tail end of what had been said.

Liz looked mutinous. She didn't want the boy who'd made the last half term so miserable to be anywhere near this excitement.

Jenny saw her expression and remembered that Liz hadn't heard of any of the reasons for Ryan's behaviour. Cupping her hand to Liz's ear, she quickly told Ryan's story, and how their happiness and success had made him feel even more miserable. Liz frowned hard, recalling all the upset, the note, and name calling. All the tears she had shed and sleepless nights, the last six weeks had been the most unpleasant of her life and not knowing why had been the worst part. Summoning all her kindness and warmth, imaging just how terrible she would feel if her parents were fighting, Liz turned to Ryan.

"Of course you must come," she said, generously, and Ryan again burst into tears, as Tony and Kate looked on, rather alarmed.

"I'm so sorry, Liz," he mumbled. Liz put her arm around him.

"It's OK."

"Right, shall we go?" said Tony. "Morton, you're under arrest for suspicion of possession of controlled drugs with intent to supply." Tony cautioned Morton, and James mouthed along, his father had taught him the caution years ago.

Morton was quiet and compliant. He helped support Ryan as a rather odd band of a police officer, four kids, one limping boy in pyjamas and a prisoner made their way along the path to the bottom of Flittermouse Cliffs. Kate had gone back up the crag to guide Dan to the abseil point, hoping she could find it in the dark.

It didn't take long before they were all standing at the bottom of Flittermouse Cliffs where, only a few days before, they'd all enjoyed rock climbing and abseiling. It seemed a lifetime ago now, so much had happened since.

Tony shone his powerful torch up and Barrie guided it. It looked different in the dark and, for a moment, he worried he'd not be able to find the place. Ah! There was an eye bolt shining in the torchlight. So along to the left, yes! There was the silver birch tree. He moved the torch beam further to the left again, and the small crevice in the cliff face appeared, at this angle, it looked little more than a crack.

"There," he said, holding the beam steady.

Barrie studied Morton closely as the crevice was illuminated. He was sure there was a flicker of alarm over his face before a neutral expression returned.

A shout from above. "Rope coming down."

Tony's radio crackled into life.

"Dan's letting the rope down," said Kate over the radio.

Tony moved everyone to one side and two lengths of red rope dropped down the cliff face, reaching the ground. James, Jenny and Liz all shone their torches up the cliff, lighting up as much of the rope as possible.

Tony stood close to Morton, silently letting him know that running was not an option.

A tall, fair haired man dressed in black police uniform, with a blue harness came into view as he began abseiling down.

"Aim for where my torch is," shouted up Tony and the man pushed his feet to take him straight towards it.

The four held their breath.

Dan stopped when he reached the crevice, tying a knot in his rope to stop him dropping any further.

Producing a torch from his belt, he shone it into the hole in the rock face.

The four watched nervously, their hearts beating fast. This was it. From Barrie's first suspicion, from the phone left in the bag, Liz's overheard conversation, all of their considerations. What would Dan find? Would it be drugs, or bats?

He seemed to be looking for ages. The silence was unbearable, the crevice was only small, it couldn't take more than a few seconds to look in. The seconds ticked by, feeling like an eternity.

"He can't be finding anything," thought Barrie, feeling pretty devastated.

Just as he was about to share his thoughts with the other three, Dan's voice was clearly heard.

"Six," he shouted, and Liz, Barrie, Jenny and James all breathed sighs of relief, realising they'd all be holding their breaths for what felt like ages.

"Go again," shouted Tony.

"Six," repeated Dan. "Six packages. Don't know what's in them, but they look like drug packages. Stand by."

There was an impatient wait as Dan took several flash photos, put on latex gloves and unfolded a large plastic evidence bag he'd had tucked into his vest.

Tony's torch clearly showed Dan removing the packages one by one and placing them carefully in a bag.

"Coming down!" he called and, untying the knot, continued down the cliff face to where Tony, Morton and the five children waited.

Unclipping himself from the rope, Dan handed the bag containing the packages to Tony to inspect.

"I think you're right, Dan," said Tony, looking at the bag carefully. "Cuff him."

Morton, his head bowed in shame, or defeat, held his arms out as Dan applied the handcuffs. The game, for him, was over.

Tony turned to the four, who were all beaming. Relieved at their suspicions being right and their efforts to solve the mystery being a success, but sad that Morton had been mixed up in a bad world.

"Well, what do you know? A right band of crime fighters you are aren't you? Excellent work, all of you. I don't know how you knew all you did, but I'm very impressed, well done."

"MRT are just going to let a stretcher down for the injured boy," Dan said to Tony, as a second man, dressed in a red jumpsuit appeared on the rope, abseiling down the cliff on Dan's line. "They'll haul him up and get him off to hospital."

That was excitement in itself for Ryan who, still profuse with apologies to the four, was strapped securely in a scoop.

"You four are my heroes!" he called, as he was carefully lifted up the cliff face.

Waving until he was out of sight, the four turned back to where Tony, Dan and Morton stood.

"We'll walk together down the path to the hostel," said Tony. "A van is meeting us there."

As they all started to walk along the path, Barrie turned and glanced back up at the cliffs for one last time.

"Well, Flittermouse Cliffs," he said, "that was your secret. I bet you'll be happier to just have bats in you from now on."

Chapter Twenty

The End of the Adventure

Exhausted from all the excitement and a serious lack of sleep, the four with Tony, Dan and Morton arrived back at the hostel just after two o'clock.

Several lights were on and Miss Martin, Mr Atkinson and David stood together at the front door anxiously, waiting for news. They looked shocked to see Morton in handcuffs, and stared with confused expressions as he was led to a waiting police van and taken away. Curtains in both dorms twitched and pupils were firmly sent back to bed until the morning.

Miss Martin, Mr Atkinson and David gathered the four inside. Miss Martin, exclaiming her relief that they were safe, left to be taken in another police car to see Ryan in the hospital.

Mr Atkinson made large steaming mugs of hot chocolate, knowing the four would be too excited for sleep and keen himself to hear their story. Taking it in turns, they told how Barrie just couldn't shake the feeling that there was something odd about Morton's behaviour at the cliffs and how Liz, overhearing the conversation, seemed to confirm that something serious was going on.

"You should have told us," said Mr Atkinson.

"We didn't think you'd believe us," said James. "Miss Martin had said she didn't care what story we came up with, after we got caught out of bounds. And I thought if you didn't believe us, and told Morton, or worse, sent us home..."

"We'd been trying to follow Morton then," added Barrie. "We'd guessed his nan was made up."

"I see. I guess I can understand your concerns. I'm just so glad you are OK," smiled Mr Atkinson, warmly. The four may have broken the rules by going out of bounds, but he couldn't help feeling extremely impressed by their courage and determination.

"I can't believe it," said David, over and over again. "All those visits to his nan, he must have gone two or three times most weeks since about June. He's only been here this season, and kept himself to himself, but I'd never have guessed he was mixed up in drugs! He was always so pleasant."

Three o'clock came and Mr Atkinson suggested they all get to bed, try to sleep and lie in till eight in the morning. Half the dorms had been woken by the police arriving and had taken some time to settle back down, so no one would be in a hurry to get up.

"I'll wait up for news from Margaret," he said, gathering up the mugs. "Miss Martin," he corrected.

The four, feeling they'd never sleep, their minds replaying the events of the night, quietly changed into their pyjamas and slid into their bunks, without waking anyone. Despite their assertions, within five minutes, they were all fast asleep.

The following morning brought news. Miss Martin had returned with Ryan, a different Ryan this time, no trace of hostility or bad temper now that his sad reason for his behaviour was out in the open. His ankle was strapped up. It had been badly sprained but wasn't broken and should heal just fine after a few weeks on crutches.

The four were relieved. None of them would have wanted Ryan to have been badly injured by following them.

As a celebration of everyone being OK, Mr Atkinson and David had set to work in the kitchen making pancakes, and everyone enjoyed a late breakfast of pancakes with syrup and mugs of hot tea. The tale of the previous night was told and retold as the other pupils all wanted to hear it, and wished that they too had been able to share the adventure. It was a very lively breakfast; in spite of the disturbed night most had experienced.

By the time the minibus was getting loaded ready to leave it was nearly lunchtime. The morning's plan had been to leave by nine o'clock and visit the castle they had seen on the beach on the way home, and Mr Atkinson said he'd arrange with the headmaster for a day trip to the castle to be held in the spring instead. That pleased Jenny, who'd been very much looking forward to it, although she wouldn't have swapped their adventure for it in a month of Sundays.

Just as the last bags were being put on, a police car arrived and Tony got out, waving to the four. He looked different in uniform and said he'd come on duty early to see them before they left.

Sitting in the lounge with the four, the teachers and David, Tony updated them all. Morton had been interviewed that morning and had confessed everything.

Struggling financially, he'd been offered the chance to make easy money. Thinking it would be a one off, he'd accepted the offer and then had found himself drawn deeper and deeper into the dark world of drugs. A place difficult to escape from, when he'd tried to back out he had been threatened with violence and hadn't known where to turn.

"He was almost relieved that we've put a stop to it," said Tony. "When those girls were hurt, he had felt physically sick, but was in with dangerous people, and under pressure to sell. Now he can hopefully work at putting his life back on the right track after we've finished with him."

"I still can't believe it," said David, wondering how a person he had lived with for the whole season had managed to lead such a double life.

"Desperate people can do strange things," replied Tony. "But he did actually ask that his thanks were passed to the four." The four looked up, surprised. "Genuinely," said Tony, smiling round at the four. "I read it in the file before coming over, your sharp eyes, ears and minds have put an end to it. He is thankful."

Arrangements were made for statements to be taken from the four over the next week and, thanking them for their outstanding courage and bravery, Tony got back into his car and drove slowly away down the track.

"What will you do now, David?" asked Barrie.

"Well, the season is over here until March next year," said David. "I guess they'll look for a replacement for Morton. In the meantime, I will tidy this place up and shut it down for the winter next week, do any repairs that are needed, then I'm off to New Zealand to work there for four months, doing something very similar to here. Oh, before I forget," David handed Mr Atkinson an envelope. "It's got the memory card in it with your week's photos."

Mr Atkinson thanked him, putting it safely in his inside coat pocket.

Liz felt quite sorry that they would be leaving David on his own, but he didn't look sad.

"He'll be OK," said Jenny, reading her friend's mind.

As they all finally piled onto the minibus for the journey back to Grey Owls, David stepped up behind.

"You know, you read about people who just seem to find adventure wherever they go."

"Yes," laughed Barrie flopping into a seat near Jenny, James and Liz. "You read about people like, he paused and the other three joined in in unison, laughing:

"Us!"

Ryan, sat at the front with his ankle propped up raised his voice.

"Three cheers for James, Jenny, Barrie and Liz!" he shouted. "Hip Hip!"

"Hooray, hooray, hooray!" chorused all on the bus, and, as David stepped back off, and Mr Atkinson lurched the minibus forward, the cheers could still be heard plainly, drowning out the noise of Mr Atkinson torturing the gearbox.

Liz, feeling the happiest she had all term, smiled at the other three. Everything had come right. There would be no more unpleasantness at school and, working together, they had managed to solve the secret of Flittermouse Cliffs.

"Do you think that will be our last adventure?" she asked the other three, reflecting on David's last words.

The three looked at her as if she'd lost her mind.

"No way!" they all said, and Liz grinned happily. She had a distinct feeling they might be right.